## Praise for Sappho's Agency

"An enjoyable foray into erotic, female-centric literature, with enough nuance and structure to serve as decent sci-fi."
—*Kirkus Reviews*

"...a complex world rich in possibilities."
—*Sci-Fi Romance Quarterly*

"Who Morning and Black actually are, accented with various sexual fetishes that become revealed, involves a mixture of political significance, advanced technology, and passionate sexual expression."
—*Alaska Women Speak*

## BOOKS BY LIZZIE NEWELL

Sappho's Agency
The Fisherman and the Sperm Thief

### Coming Soon
Tristan Bay Accord

# By Lizzie Newell

lizzienewell.com
**Anchorage, Alaska**

9138 Arlon St., Ste. A3-625
Anchorage, Alaska
99507

Library of Congress Control Number: 2015901433
ISBN: 978-1-942528-01-02
eISBN: 978-1-942528-00-5


Version 2.0.2

# DEDICATION

To my friend Sappho. You inspire me with your faith
and resilience.

# ACKNOWLEDGMENTS

I could not have written this without the inspirations of conventions and writers' conferences: Kachemak Bay Writers' Conference, North Words Writers Symposium, Norwescon, Emerald City Writers' Conference, Alaska Writers Guild Conference, and RWA Annual Conference. Thank you to Rebecca Goodrich for early developmental editing and for discussing writing at odd hours. Thanks go to Deb Vanasse, Dana Stabenow, and Andromeda Romano-Lax for excellent classes through 49 Writers. To Tam Linsey, thank you for leading the way on self-publishing. Thank you to beta readers: Raven Demers, Judith Conte, and Morgan Grey. Finally thanks to go to Cassie Cox of Red Adept Editing.

# CONTENTS

# Foreplay

M Y INSEMINATION PHALLUS ready, I touched our client with a gloved hand. I remained professional, a woman doing her job. My partner, Daisy, whispered and stroked the girl's hair, comforting the girl as she knelt with her head pillowed on Daisy's ample breasts.

"I miss him so much." The girl's voice quavered.

"Of course you do. And you'll have his baby," Daisy said, caressing the girl's shoulder.

"A boy?"

"A boy like his father or a girl as brave and beautiful as her mother," Daisy whispered.

So courageous, this young woman. For two years, she'd fought to obtain a few spoonfuls of her sweetheart's semen, his last living remains. Clans commonly banked the sperm of their young men but were loath to part with the samples. That fluid was now in the chamber of my phallus.

He'd been a sailor boy, she a student. They'd decided to wait to marry until after she finished her studies. The day after she'd completed her thesis, he died at sea.

She quivered under my touch. With a finger, I parted her inner lips.

"He's watching over you," Daisy said.

I eased the tip of the phallus into her. She gasped as I slid the shaft into place.

Daisy's arms encircled the girl's shoulders. "A beautiful baby."

One hand on the girl's haunches, I drew my hips back, withdrawing my phallus ever so slightly. She moaned, and I pushed, rocking, seeking that delicious spot inside her. *There. There. Oh yes!* With a gasp, she arched her back. I slipped a finger to the release mechanism and increased my pace. She moaned in time to my movement.

Daisy held up a finger, signaling. *Wait. Wait. Now!*

With a deep thrust, I activated the trigger, sending the hard-won fluid into her. She shuddered, her breathing rapid, her skin glowing with sweat. She gasped then let out a sigh of contentment.

"Rest." Daisy slipped out from under the girl. "He would be proud of you."

Daisy placed a pillow under the girl's head and covered her with a quilt. Daisy and I left the room. With the door shut, I pulled off my gloves.

"Incredible! She's incredible. That was perfect. You were perfect." I gave Daisy a squeeze. "Thank you. Thank you for finding her. The scandal sheets! To think you found her in the scandal sheets."

The girl and her quest had become a cause célèbre in the gossip news. Daisy, after reading about the girl, had dropped hints in appropriate places to refer her to our agency. A mysterious benefactor, using the name

"Littlemara," had prevailed on the sailor boy's clan to yield the packet. We'd done it, fulfilled the hopes of that brave young woman.

The pregnancy would take. I felt sure of it. Working together, Daisy and I had honed our technique until we'd achieved excellence and received payment to match.

But for this girl, we'd waived all fees.

# CHAPTER 01
## The Dame

A DAME STOPPED before our door, just outside my window. One-way glass. What a great investment. She was not my type—quite snooty actually—face pinched, grumpy, a woman who surely hadn't been laid recently. She was clearly a dame, one of those mature women reeking of clan politics. Her smock, or maybe more rightly her tunic, was a sort of high-class neutral brown, no indication of clan. Most likely this dame was hiding her identity, chagrined that she, a woman of status, had been unable to make arrangements for a man on her own.

I welcomed her in, and she glanced around my office at the photos of mothers and babies on the wall, at the stud albums on a low table, at my desk and dimmed planning screen, seemingly assessing it all and finding it lacking. Now that she was inside, I could see the subtle herringbone pattern on her smock, understated, excessively tasteful. A traditional fabric panel on the front of her smock hid pockets for com-set and tools. From the gray in her hair and her slack chin, I judged she was nearing menopause.

I bowed politely. "Welcome. What are you about?"

Her answer was just as standard but brief. "The tide."

"The water is lovely today." I smiled.

In her own time, she would surely broach the subject on her mind. My clients were often reticent at first. And a middle-aged woman who had delayed childbearing would naturally feel awkward seeking professional help.

"Would you like some refreshment?"

She nodded, so I stood and poured raspberry leaf tea from a samovar into a cup. "Sweetener?"

"Please."

I stirred in a spoonful of malt syrup and gave her the cup and a saucer. I filled a cup for myself. Leaving it behind, I went into the kitchen to give her time to become comfortable. From the cold cupboard, I removed a plate of cress sandwiches—triangles of bread with the crusts removed, the sort of thing she might like. She was still standing when I returned with napkins and the plate of dainty finger food.

"Make yourself at home." I gestured with the plate toward our intimate arrangement of couches and chairs.

She chose a chair.

I smiled. "A sandwich?"

She selected one and held it between her thumb and forefinger. I set the plate on the table, sat on the couch, and sipped my own cup of tea.

She narrowed her lips and drew her eyebrows together. "What is your policy on privacy?" Her glare focused on a photo of a young woman holding a chubby baby.

"I can assure you we have the greatest respect for client confidentiality. We are noted for our discretion."

"So I've been told." The woman sampled her sandwich

and grimaced. "But tell me. Those photos—have you been given permission to put them on display?"

"Would you like to see documentation?" I popped a whole sandwich triangle in my mouth and washed it down with tea. I smiled and nodded at a photo. "Just look at those dimples, the baby fat. His mother and grandmother are so proud. They sent the picture as a thank-you." Daisy and I considered ourselves mothers many times over. I was a certified midwife, and our clients stayed in touch with us, often seeking advice on their children and relationships.

"I suppose so," she said. "I'm interested in your services for my niece, but I do not want her displayed in your little gallery."

"We can provide any level of privacy you wish. Here at Sappho's Agency, our clients come first." I cradled the warm cup in my hands. "Tell me about your niece. How can we be of service?" I set my cup aside and gestured toward a brochure tablet. "We have a variety of packages. We specialize in assisting first-time mothers, but many of our clients are so pleased that they return to us for their second and third child."

Despite my enthusiasm, the brochure remained on the table untouched. She nibbled her sandwich.

"Do you have a father in mind?" I flicked a stud catalog cube, activating revolving images of men. "We don't have a sperm bank here, but we have catalogs available and can refer you." Stud catalogues couldn't be accessed without a referral. "What sort of genetics would your niece like? Musical talent? Intelligence? A good head for business?" I dangled possibilities before her. "Political acumen?"

The dame dusted her fingers. "That won't be necessary.

We've already selected a father."

If a woman had chosen a man and he was agreeable, they usually could handle matters quite well on their own. Most of our clientele were women unable to find suitable husbands. The Fenrian Archipelago had a shortage of men. Too many of them died in fishing and boating accidents—risky behavior. Actually the entire planet had a shortage of men, but we drew our clientele primarily from the Fenrian Archipelago.

What was this dame doing in my front room office? What was the hitch in her plans?

"Very well." I shut off the revolving studs and folded my hands. "How may we help you?"

"My niece is a very special young lady, highly thought of in our clan." The dame reached for her cup.

"Yes. And?"

She sipped. "The young man is highly placed in his clan."

High status? Usually not a problem.

"Our clan and his clan are not—how shall I say it?— are not on the best of terms."

"Oh?"

"We would like this liaison to have no lasting consequences."

I gave her a glare as haughty as her own. "A baby is a lasting consequence."

"Political consequences. We would like for neither my niece nor the young man to know the other's identity."

"In that case, may I recommend artificial insemination?"

"No, no. Not for my niece nor this man. The situation requires that they ah... that they..."

"That they actually have sex," I finished, unsympathetic

to her prudishness. "We can assist with arrangements. However, I must be certain this man agrees to fathering a child and that appropriate permission has been obtained from his clan." Occasionally women attempted to trick a man into fathering a child, a deception I refused to take part in.

"We have tacit approval," the dame said. "Outright permission would be politically risky for both clans."

I countered, "Assisting in the conception of a child without permission from the father's clan puts us in a risky situation, both legally and ethically. We need documented permission."

"Please don't misunderstand." The dame removed a tambour screen from her front pocket. The traditional reader screen folded to the size of two knitting needles. "We have a legal team advising. They assure us that nothing we're proposing is illegal, and we have plenty of documentation." She stretched open the screen to display a rolling listing of records, far too many for me to examine immediately.

"I'll have to speak with our lawyer," I said.

"Our lawyers can speak to your lawyer."

Imagine that, a lawyer convention, a full legal team, arranging the girl's love life.

"I'd prefer to speak with the couple," I said. "Find out what they want."

From her pouch pocket, the dame removed a richly embossed folder nearly the size of the pocket and opened the folder to display a photocard. "This is she."

The young woman stood on the deck of a ship, white rails behind her, the sky and sea azure blue. Her brown eyes sparkled, and her tan skin had the rosy blush of youth.

"Is she of age?" I asked.

"Two-dozen years old." The woman offered a second card. "The man."

He seemed handsome enough: black hair, thick eyebrows, and his dark eyes rimmed with black.

I pointed toward his eyes. "It seems he has black mucus membranes."

"A marker of genetic excellence," she said.

So I'd been told. But I remained unconvinced that black gums and the like led to healthy children. I didn't find the markings attractive myself.

Flicking my thumb above the image, I activated it. The man turned. A network of welts laced the back of his head. Seaguard members bore such markings, the scars a sign of a direct neural interface. "Is he Seaguard?" I asked.

"The best."

I set aside the photo. Seaguard could easily run searches through countless catalogs of information only available to them. "His neural interface creates complications. Maintaining anonymity will be nearly impossible."

"But not impossible." The woman wagged her finger. "Your business has an excellent reputation. I'm sure you can handle it."

Her sudden shift to flattery unnerved me. "I'll have to speak with my partner. May I show her these?" I reached for the photocards. Daisy had a good instinct for people.

"You may." The woman stood, her tea and sandwiches left behind. "Consider with care. If you have any questions, please contact me." From her shoulder pocket, she removed a bi-fold com-unit.

I pulled mine from my shoulder pocket, and our units did their little exchange of information.

"You understand—we prefer to withhold our clan name," she said. "I've given you contact codes to reach our legal team. They can ratify our good intent and vouch for us." She pocketed her unit.

I accompanied her to the front door, and we said our good-byes. As soon as she was out the door, I flicked a finger above my planning screen to access my calendar then input the date by signaling numbers with my fingers, thumb out for the number one and across the palm for six. Our business ebbed and flowed with the three-year lunar cycle. In the low tide years, Daisy and I assisted young men contributing to clan sperm banks, but with the moons coming into alignment, our clientele had predominantly become women seeking pregnancy.

My favorite clients were young women. They often came to us with very little experience. I taught them to respect and appreciate their bodies. Every woman was unique, and her reproductive experience should be tailored to her individual needs, a celebration of who she was mentally, physically, and spiritually. Daisy and I could arrange anything from virgin births to raucous orgies. Not that there was much call for virgin birth— it required anesthesia for both insemination and the caesarian delivery. I'd very much like to work with the young woman in the photo.

"Hailing Daisy." My unit recognized her name and made the call. "Sappho here," I said when she answered. "I just received an unusual case. I'd like to know what you think."

Daisy burst through the door, a canvas bag of groceries slung over her arm. "What do you have for me this time?"

"A fusty old dame," I said, teasing her.

Daisy pouted, her expression playful.

I added, "Arranging a direct cover liaison for her niece. Except I'm not sure the girl is actually her niece. The liaison is supposed to be anonymous."

The tail of Daisy's turquoise smock swished as she carried the groceries into the kitchen. "Have they chosen a man?"

I followed her. "He's Seaguard. That's about all I know about him. The dame has a delusion he won't figure out the girl's name." I snorted a laugh.

Daisy set the bag on the table. "Maybe he already knows." From the bag, she removed a basket of blueberries and a bottle of fermented milk.

I opened the cold cupboard to stow the food. Daisy placed a package of dried anchovies in a cupboard. I loved her full bouncing breasts, her swelling hips, the curve of her thighs, and the way her smock rose when she reached for the high shelf. For all her sweetness, Daisy could never be happy with access to only one woman, or one man for that matter. She liked her variety, but amazingly, she remained with me as my partner.

I shut the cold cupboard door. "The girl looks quite young, but the 'aunt' assures me the girl is an adult."

We went into the front room. Snow fell in the lane, feathery flakes drifting slowly and melting on wet cobblestones. The spring equinox had come and gone, but winter had yet to release its grip.

I rolled my chair to my desk. The photocards remained beside my planning screen. I glanced at the girl's image.

Our potential client had such a look of innocence in her shy smile and bright eyes.

Oh, yes, I'd prefer artificial insemination for her. Direct cover introduced so many risks to a young woman. Often the male was so self-conscious he couldn't get it up. Or he was rough, most often the result of inexperience. If he had experience, he could carry diseases. With artificial insemination, we were better able to control pathogens. I set both photocards upright, their covers partly open. My chair creaked as I leaned back.

Daisy reclined on my desk, supporting herself with one arm. Her soft curls, dark against her bright smock, grazed her shoulders. She glanced at the photos and her tongue skimmed her lips. Then her eyes widened, and she seized the image of the man. "This is him?"

"Aye." I hadn't expected Daisy to be all that impressed by his unusual pigmentation.

Daisy held up the folio, the cover flapping open. "This is Reolo Comryez!"

"Who?" I'd heard of Clan Comryez but not this Reolo fellow. "Is he a pirate?" The clan had a reputation for shipwrecking and ongoing feuds. I hummed the tune of a folksong that told of Clan Comryez and their legendary battles.

Daisy laughed. "Sapph, you really should read the scandal sheets." She waved the photocard. "Reolo Comryez, the most eligible—and untouchable—bachelor in the Fenrian Islands. They say he's taken a vow of celibacy. His mother forced it on him as a condition of his appointment as lord of Comryez Pass. His uncle died of a heart attack, and Reolo was next in line. I think it was last summer."

"But why celibacy?" Either the mother had approved

the liaison and the rumor was false, or she didn't know about the planned liaison.

"Because he's Comryez. Comryez has always required celibacy from their magnate. They've made a tradition of it, just like their grudges. By the way, his mother's name is Stink Lily, named after a flower which smells like manure." The bridge of Daisy's nose wrinkled. "Odd clan. They follow their own weird customs."

I took back the photocard and returned to the topic. "The girl's aunt was quite concerned about confidentiality."

"With good reason," Daisy said. "If journalists get a whiff of this, they'll be all over us."

I closed the folio, covering the man's image. "The case is ethically murky. The girl's clan has only tacit permission from his clan. I'm thinking we should turn down the case."

"Are you kidding? Pass up a chance to work with that?" She flipped open the cover. "Isn't he luscious? I could lick him all over. Wouldn't you like to know what he looks like under—"

"Daisy. I haven't accepted yet."

"I'd like to get my hands on his—"

"Daisy! They've requested direct cover."

"He's just so tempting. Mmm mmm." She sighed. "Direct cover. They would require that for him. Rumor has it he can't get it up on his own."

"That's ridiculous. How would the gossip mongers know anyway?" My chair squeaked.

Daisy clasped the photo card. "Word is his father was Teakh Noahee. You know, the most expensive stud in Fenrian history? The one who went rogue and kidnapped his own children?"

"Our man can't be one of those children. He's too young."

"Here's where the story gets good," Daisy said. "You see, right before Teakh was executed —"

"The Littlemara deaths were accidental."

"Or maybe they escaped and left the planet. Whichever. Right before Teakh was caught, he sneaked into Comryez Pass and impregnated Stink Lily. That's one story. The other is that Stink Lily sneaked into his prison cell to steal his oh-so-valuable semen."

"Or maybe someone like Daisy went from the prison cell to Comryez Pass. Or maybe she stole it earlier."

Daisy blew at a strand of her escaping hair. "In old stud catalogs, Teakh was billed as, get this, 'only able to perform under conditions of direct cover.' Supposedly he had the genetic profile of the perfect father: innately monogamous, nurturing, and self-sacrificing. That's the shine in the catalogs anyway. They talked him up for his genetics but left out his photo. If he looked anything like Reolo here..." Daisy whistled.

I proffered the other photocard. "So what about the girl?"

"A very fortunate young lady."

I searched the girl's dimples and brown hair for signs of clan or status. "Who do you think she is?" She wore a simple brown student's smock, collar buttoned, hood thrown back. The railing behind her could have belonged to a ferry. Nothing about her indicated status on par with a Seaguard Lord, even one with a mother named Stink Lily.

"Comryez isn't going to permit any children by that delicious man." Daisy's tongue swept over her lips. "The aunt is lying."

"And you've been reading gossip news," I said. "What Comryez claim and what they do may be two different things. The rumor may be an oversimplification. Rumors often are."

"Maybe. But Comryez has always kept the existence of resulting children a secret and avoided entangling alliances. Comryez is beholden to no one. Or so they say."

"Plenty of Comryez men have married and fathered children," I said.

"Not Lord Comryez Pass. He just might decide he liked his wife's kids better than his nieces and nephews. Imagine that!" Daisy scooted off my desk, and her feet thumped the floor. "If we accept this case, we'll be making history."

Conservative fear mongers warned that the entire clan system would end if men took care of their own children. Such a radical change would pit nephew against son for inheritance and force women into restrictive marriages in order to ensure paternity. It seemed to me, though, that folks could use paternity tests if there were any doubts.

"No, we won't," I said. "If we do it right, no word will get out to be written up, even by your scandal sheets."

Daisy leaned both her hands on my desk. "Then we're accepting the case?"

"It depends on what we find out about the girl and the girl's clan."

"So what do you have on them?" Daisy eyed the photocards.

"A clan at odds with Comryez."

Daisy snorted. "What clan isn't at odds with Comryez? Offhand, I'd say it's a long-term investment. The girl's clan is trying to produce a stud as valuable as Teakh Noahee." Daisy paced, finger to her plump lips. "We don't know for sure Reolo was sired by Teakh. Teakh and his offspring were noted mostly for their loyalty. Which means..." She pivoted.

"Is the girl actually the woman's niece? Or is she a poor girl with good genes?" I asked. "Possibly a surrogate. So what's the game?"

"I'll ask around at the docks." Daisy grabbed her parka and went out the door.

She didn't go beyond flirting in her effort to get the scoop. Although she could flirt with the best of them. We made a good team.

## CHAPTER 02
## Our Lawyer

IN HER STOCKING feet, Daisy padded into the front office. "The dame arrived by esskip taxi out of Fennako City, and the pilot had a bite to eat at Fillie's Café."

I rolled back my chair from the legal documents displayed on my planning screen. I'd been looking through the packet left by the dame. "That could mean about anything."

"It means she has loads of money for this project. She, or her clan, paid for the flight from Fennako City." Daisy glanced at my planning screen. "What have you found in those legal briefs?"

"A lot of lawyer-shine. I sent a message to our lawyer. She'll look it over for us. One thing about legal briefs—they aren't brief."

Daisy rolled her eyes.

"You like other kinds of briefs," I said.

"Aye. Briefs or boxers or none at all." Daisy drummed fingers against her thigh.

I gave her a squeeze. "I like none at all."

She moved closer, in easy reach for me to nibble on her ear. She relaxed in my embrace.

In the afternoon, Daisy and I met with our lawyer via remote.

She regarded us from my planning screen. "I've looked over these documents, and they're all in order. You should have no fears in taking this case. The woman's clan accepts all legal responsibility."

"The girl appears to be extremely young," I said. "She could be easily manipulated by her clan into acting as a surrogate."

"As part of a eugenics program," Daisy added.

The lawyer laughed. "An interesting theory. Are you perhaps a devotee of Littlemara philosophy?"

The name kept coming up, first as the benefactor who'd assisted with the sailor boy's semen, then in association with our most recent client, the Littlemara boys who'd been kidnapped by their father.

"Didn't know they had a philosophy." I shrugged. "I just know that people anonymously performing charitable deeds use that name."

"Two supreme court justices have signed off on these documents. Also Annon Noahee, the human rights lawyer who represented the Littlemara boys."

"Noahee?" Daisy asked, leaning against my desk. "Any relationship to the stud Teakh Noahee?"

"His sister actually. Be assured, you should have no hesitation in accepting this case. If you feel that either party is being coerced, you are free to end the arrangement, as are they. You'll still be paid a tidy sum, paid in halibut."

"But if they don't know the identity of their partner," I said, "they're incapable of giving informed consent."

"The law is satisfied on that issue. You're free to make up your own mind. And if you do your usual excellent work, they'll know the important things about each other."

"It's not possible for them to remain anonymous to each other," I said. "Daisy knew the man right away. Identified him from a photo."

Daisy smiled and nodded.

"Then don't let her see his face," our lawyer said.

"Masked? I don't think it'll work."

"Give them the pretense of anonymity anyway."

"Then you think they might know?" I asked.

In answer, our lawyer smiled. "Congratulations. If you pull it off, it's something to be proud of. That they chose you is a tribute to your skill and good reputation."

The screen blinked off.

Daisy removed a handscreen from her pocket. "Who's the girl?"

"She's more than likely to show up on your scandal sheets. You tell me," I said.

The fun thing about matrilineal clans, for Daisy anyway, was that paternity was usually secret or at least private. Those who loved gossip endlessly speculated about who fathered whom. Daisy knew more about paternity than almost anyone, but she still enjoyed the sport.

She opened her tambour frame, stretching the screen taut. "Let me have that photo."

Daisy stepped out of the shower, her body wet and her hair in arabesque tendrils. "Do you remember our lawyer mentioning Littlemara philosophy?"

Faced with such a scrumptious view, I couldn't remember anything. "Sure. Anything you say."

"I looked it up." She reached for a towel and wound it around her head as a turban. "Rockfish Littlemara is the philosopher. He claims to be the son of Teakh Noahee, but no one knows for sure." She dried herself with a second towel, passing it between her legs.

"It's probably just an alias." I swallowed and looked away. "Someone afraid to use his own name."

"Anyway, he believes Seaguard men are being exploited."

"Exploited? Seaguard has it good. They fly esskips. A lot of them are rich. Women fall all over them. Your scandal sheets love them. How often have we assisted with fantasies involving sex with Seaguard men? Even the men get off on it."

"It's the Seaguard kit." Standing on one foot, Daisy lifted the other and pointed her toes. "Jackboots. Mmm mmm."

I laughed. "Janeboots. That's for me."

"Seriously though," Daisy said, drying her hair, her raised arms lifting her breasts. "They get neuros as children and have no say in the operation. Then they're brainwashed and forced into a hierarchical organization. Marriage and sexual contacts—all carefully controlled."

"But left to their own devices, men engage in too much risk," I said. "They're the weaker sex."

She reached for her robe and wrapped her tender curves in soft terrycloth. "Sapph, don't give me that shine. Men can be just as responsible as women. And many women take risks too, stupid risks."

"I suppose so." I stroked her thigh, lifting her wrap above her hip.

She slapped my hand away. "According to this Rockfish fellow, you and I are part of this exploitation."

"Now that's shine." With a swift pull, I removed the wrap and dropped it on the floor.

THE DAME CONTACTED us by remote the next day. Daisy still had been unable to find anything on the girl, but the couple intrigued us. We didn't talk money. Our lawyer would take care of that. Daisy and I had become so successful, we only accepted clients we liked, no longer using ability to pay as the only criterion.

"Now understand," the dame said, seated in a distant office, "we must protect my niece's identity. No one should see her arrive or leave."

Was she thinking of draping the girl in enveloping veils? As if that wouldn't attract attention.

"We can arrange to meet with her at a secluded retreat," I offered. "But we can't promise she won't be seen while arriving."

"We'll secure transportation," the dame said.

"We'd like to meet with her first and have enough time to really get to know her. Ideally in multiple sessions."

"That fits our timeline," the dame said. "You'll have plenty of time to work with her. However, contact between her and this man must remain brief. We request that you make this case your top priority, your only priority."

"I have other clients scheduled."

"Just make sure it doesn't interfere."

I raised my eyebrows at Daisy.

She said, "Sapph, if problems come up, we can drop it. That is true. Yes?" She smiled at the dame.

"Any party may end the contract at any time."

The screen blinked off. I doubted it would be that simple, not with Comryez involved. Danna help us! Eugenicists, sperm thieves, and radicals.

## CHAPTER 03
## Cozy Cove

Mist drifted above the cove, the water as smooth and reflective as a mirror. The air was cool and the sky tinged with pink. The esskip delivering the girl to Cozy Cove was nowhere in sight. We'd arranged to meet with her in monthly three-day sessions during the waning of Luna Majora, the traditional time for initiation of relationships. The liaison with the man would be during the full moon.

Gravel crunched under our feet as we walked down the sloping path to the floating dock. We'd rented and prepared the cottage for the girl's arrival, cleaning, decorating, and stocking the cupboards with foods that were delicious but easily prepared. We liked to use Cozy Cove for clients who requested complex scenarios. The place was secluded, and its extensive grounds were kept natural and rustic.

A bird chirped. The dock swayed slightly under our feet, the undulation disturbing the calm surface of the water. From the dock, I looked back at the shore. The tide was out, exposing mottled green bladder wrack. A jet of water squirted from the sand—a clam clearing its siphon. Built on a rise overlooking the cove, the cottage remained shrouded in trees and shadows. Behind the cottage, trees and ferns clung to the granite face of a ridge.

Arm-in-arm, Daisy and I waited. Through the low fog, the craft came, a gray esskip skimming over the water, scattering the mist, and marring the perfection of the mirror with the wind of her passage.

"Not a commercial taxi," I said.

By law, each esskip had an identification number, including clan prefix, displayed prominently on the tail. This esskip, painted a clandestine gray, had none.

"I'd say Fennako," Daisy said, pushing back her hair. "They're the only clan that can get away with an unmarked craft."

The esskip extended landing skis and hydroplaned, wings open, until she slowed and settled on the water. She folded her wings and pivoted, her gray nose directed toward us, her wake sending the dock trembling.

We held our breaths as the canopy opened, revealing the first view of our client, a brown-haired girl in the back seat. I knew her from the photo. Strangely enough, the pilot was also a woman. Female esskip pilots were extremely rare, but I averted my gaze. Daisy, not as polite, was staring.

As the craft drifted into the dock, the girl stood, a line in her hand. The surface of the craft had the resilience of skin as the wings folded along the fuselage. The girl jumped lightly ashore and secured the line to a cleat as naturally as if she'd worked as a deckhand. Her life vest matched the clandestine gray of the esskip's skin, and that was as odd as the stealth esskip and the woman flying it.

Fishermen wore brightly colored life vests so they would be seen. Seaguard generally wore vests that advertised clan affiliation.

The girl straightened, dusted her hands, and took a breath, her eyes bright. "Well?"

I greeted her. "Welcome. What are you about?"

She smiled, and her face dimpled. "The tide. And mooring an esskip. Pleased to meet you." She bowed.

"Sappho here, and my partner Daisy." I also bowed.

"You can call me..." She looked about at the mist, now sunlight touched. "How about Morning?"

"Morning, then," I said. The name fit her.

She glanced at the woman pilot. "Just a moment."

The female pilot stood and handed out a duffle. Morning accepted it and dropped the bag on the dock. She removed her life vest and threw it into the backseat then untied the line and tossed it to the pilot.

"Tide carry you." The pilot coiled the line. "Danna guide you." Large sunglasses hid the woman's expression.

"Thank you." For a moment, Morning's lip quivered. "See you later."

The canopy closed. Morning watched as the esskip taxied away and, wings extended, rose on step, water spraying from the craft's hydrofoil skis. The landing skis retracted as the craft disappeared through the fog, as if she were a mysterious gray dove.

Only when the esskip was gone did the girl turn back to us. "I'm ready."

"Come up to the house," Daisy said. "Breakfast is waiting."

The three of us walked up the gravel path to the cottage. Birch trees overhung a veranda looking out on the cove. We went up the steps to the veranda and into the kitchen, a room with a high ceiling and clay-work walls pierced by clerestory lunettes above mullioned windows. A dining nook contained four chairs placed around a wooden card table.

Morning leaned against a counter, watching me as I cooked up omelets and fried bacon. Beyond the windows, the sun rose on a spring day with leaves coming out, golden green with newness. We carried plates to the veranda to dine under an ancient birch tree. Its peeling trunk angled over the deck, and newly sprouted leaves clung to its black branches. Morning ate with gusto, consuming an omelet, bacon, and a taste of everything else. Not knowing her preferences, we'd provided cheese, pastries, clabber, and smoked haddock as well as toasted oats.

"Please feel comfortable." Sitting across the table from Morning, I delivered my usual introduction to our methods. "There isn't anything you have to do. Daisy and I would like to get to know you, to discover your desires and fantasies. Please understand that we respect client confidentiality. We will hold private anything you share with us and anything that occurs in these sessions. You are free to leave at any time. Do you have a com-unit?" I touched my own microphone and speakers secured in my shoulder pocket.

"Aye." She tapped behind her ear, an odd mannerism. "And I... uh... I have transport standing by."

"The pilot?" Daisy asked, always nosy.

Morning declined to answer.

"You may have fantasies which you may wish to act out," I said. "We can assist you, but our relationship must be one of respect for all. Go ahead and pick a safeword, something you'll not say accidentally. When you say this word, we will know you're not acting and are serious in requests for the play to cease. Promise me—if something makes you uncomfortable and you wish to stop, you'll let us know."

Morning nodded, wiped her hands on a napkin, and held up her right hand to touch mine, concluding the deal. "I choose sassafras."

I continued with my usual review of expectations. "I'd like to ask some questions. There are no right or wrong answers."

"Go ahead."

"Why do you want to have a baby?"

Morning sat back, puzzlement in her eyes as if no one had ever bothered to ask her. "I must have a daughter. It's my duty."

Daisy's mouth opened, then she straightened and popped it shut.

*Don't say anything, Daisy. Play it cool.* I clasped my hands, not speaking of our suspicions. "Tell me. Is it important to do your duty?"

"It is to me," Morning said.

Good answer. She'd spoken for herself with no suggestion of coercion.

"But what do you want?" I asked. "What would you want if you had no duty?"

"I don't know." Morning shrugged, wisps of her hair brushing her collar.

Had she truly never considered her own desires?

"Let's find out," I said. "These three days, your duty is only to yourself. To whatever you truly want."

"But I want him. I want to meet him. I want to have his child."

I frowned. No woman should receive her entire identity and happiness from a man. "Why?"

"I just do."

"Let's consider your child's gender," I said. "We have several methods for increasing the likelihood of a female child. Unfortunately, the more reliable the method, the less reliable it is for getting pregnant."

"Then either a boy or girl is fine," Morning said.

"Good. Now, about our methods. Our best success in achieving conception has been when the prospective mother enjoys an orgasm. We use natural methods of inducing ovulation. I don't mean to shine, but we've become rather good at discovering just what a girl might like." I smiled. I had little hard evidence that an orgasm increased the likelihood of ovulation, but I still believed that a woman should enjoy the experience of conceiving a child.

Morning frowned, hands in her lap.

"Daisy and I will be providing you the most intimate of assistance during the most sacred of acts. Are you comfortable with that?"

"What do you mean?" Morning fidgeted, picking at her nails.

I spoke plainly. "When you encounter your man, you're going to have an orgasm, and we're going to help. Hands-on assistance in the room. Possibly in bed with you. Whatever you need. We might touch you in ways only a partner or spouse would normally touch you."

"I suppose it's all right," she said.

Her hesitation concerned me. "You don't have to do anything unless you want to. Understand nobody will touch you in that way without your permission."

She nodded. "Aye."

I remained unconvinced of her assent. "We've been instructed to arrange a liaison with a man you do not know, and you will remain anonymous to the father of your child. Neither of you will ever know the other's name or identity. How do you feel about that?"

"But I do know him," Morning said. "I don't know his name, and we've never met in person. But..." She stroked her knee. "I feel him. A sense of him." Her eyes became dreamy.

Good Danna! An imaginary lover. I'd have to take care with the girl or she'd face crushing disappointment. A real man could never live up to a young girl's fantasies. Neither could a real woman for that matter.

"What do you sense about him?" I asked.

Daisy watched like a green-eyed cat, all restrained eagerness.

Morning's eyes snapped into focus. "Sassafras."

I forced myself to look away from Daisy, to focus instead on the new leaves on the trees. Surely Daisy, eager to speculate, could barely contain herself, but out of respect for Morning, I remained cool.

"More fruit salad?" I smiled.

"Please."

MORNING PROVED TO be an energetic hiker as we toured the grounds. The place remained natural and rustic. She peered into the boathouse, which contained canoes and a small sailboat. Then we walked up along the creek, a bright stream babbling over rocks as it flowed toward the ocean. Bracken and moss grew beside the path.

I dropped behind with Daisy. We stood on a needle-strewn path in the dappled shade of trees.

"She's Fennako. I'm sure of it," Daisy whispered.

"What about the woman pilot?" I asked.

"Now that is unusual. And with those sunglasses? She

must be in the scandal sheets somewhere."

"Her mother?" I asked.

"You noticed the resemblance. The same round face and dimples," Daisy said. She and I had become proficient at completing each other's thoughts.

"What are you gals waiting for?" Morning paused on the trail. She stood backlit by sunlight filtering through trees.

"An interesting plant," I said, searching the ground for an appropriate subject. "The way these ferns unfurl. Intriguing."

Daisy smirked and whispered, "Intriguing?"

The ferns were a weak excuse for our dallying. We caught up.

"There's a hot spring up here." Daisy led through the trees, spruce and hemlock, her rounded butt swinging.

At a creek bend, the current rushed against a cliff streaked by white minerals. Nearby, a pool of water steamed, smelling of sulfur. Last time we'd been there, a row of stones had directed cold water from the stream into the pool.

Daisy pulled her shoes off and dipped in a toe. "Ouch! Too hot."

"Give me a hand," I said to Morning. She helped me move rocks, increasing the flow of cold water.

Daisy stirred the water with her hand. "I think that's about right. Only one way to find out." She stripped off her clothing and stepped in. "Come on. It's nice."

Morning took off her shoes, rolled up her leggings, and waded into the shallow outwash. My clothing in a heap, I stepped in and lowered myself into the pool. The temperature, at first painfully hot, eased to pleasure. It occurred to me that this was the nature of pleasure. It existed on the boundary of agony, where the current of joy meets the cliff of pain.

Relaxing in the warmth, I leaned against a rock with my arm around Daisy's soft shoulder. Patterns of light shimmered on the sandy bottom and on our legs, foreshortened by the rippled surface.

Morning held her shoes and socks in one hand. "Do I have to take my clothing off?"

"Whatever you want." I kept my voice deliberately casual. At that early stage, the girl could be easily frightened. We needed her to trust us.

She sat on a rock, her knees up, only her feet in the pool. The nearby stream babbled, and a bird trilled, besotted with spring.

"This is the life," I said.

Morning wiggled her toes, distorted through the clear water. "I'd like to go fishing. There's trout in the creek. I saw some."

Daisy raised her eyebrows. "Fishing? How daring."

"Commercial fishing would be daring," Morning said. "Not fly-fishing, and that's what I do."

According to tradition, women didn't fish. In the dark ages, too many women died in fishing accidents. The prophet Catherine Smith, the mother of the first queen, had taught that women should work on land, have few children, and provide those children with good educations. But women frequently broke the taboo on fishing, and I was no traditionalist.

"There might be a rod in the boathouse." I tried to recall exactly what was in the dim storage shed.

"There is. I saw it, along with some tackle." A shy smile

danced across Morning's face. "Is it all right if I use it? I have a fishing permit, and I contacted the local Seaguard magnate. He gave me the go-ahead. He recommends using crystal eggs or roe bugs."

"Well, go right ahead," I said. "Whatever you want. We're here for you."

"I'll get the rod and tackle later. Maybe after lunch." She plucked a blade of grass. "So tell me. How did you two meet?"

Daisy laid a finger on her plump lower lip. "When we were students. I didn't know what to study. I really only had two interests: boys—"

"And boys," I added.

"Also matchmaking," Daisy said.

I elbowed her. "That's because you couldn't have all the boys to yourself."

"If only I could." Daisy sighed. "So I set up my friends with boys I liked."

"Vicarious enjoyment," I explained.

"I tried going into matchmaking for real," Daisy said. "You know, working with clan breeding programs. But eww! It's all charts and statistics and looking at family trees back to the nth generation. Then Sappho shows up in one of my classes."

"Human genetics," I said. "I was studying to be a midwife." We'd met in a seminar, and I couldn't take my eyes off her, a goddess of abundance.

Wavelets lapped Daisy's breasts. "Here was this girl with no interest in boys. I mean, none at all. I thought women did it with each other only when no men were available. So I set her up on a date with this really good-looking guy."

"What was the guy's name? I don't recall," I said.

"Mort. I went with him to help things along. Thought I'd fix her up."

"She sure did. I went for Daisy instead." I nuzzled her shoulder.

She snuggled against me, her hair soft on my cheek. "We never looked back. Best decision I ever made. Left to my own devices, I'd end up with a zillion kids, and I don't like them that well. I mean, they're cute, but only when they're somebody else's."

"We make a good team," I added, patting Daisy's arm.

"I mostly handle the men," Daisy said. "Assisting with sperm donation. I get to do lots of men. Danna! I love them."

"And I love Daisy." I gave her a squeeze. "How about you, Morning? What kind of work do you do?"

She set her hand against her ear, as she seemed to do when she was thinking. "I'm in law enforcement."

"Really?" Daisy said. "You don't look like a cop."

"So what does a cop look like?" I asked.

"Well, there's our village cop. She looks like someone's aunt," Daisy said.

"She is your aunt," I said.

"You know what I mean. She's getting kind of thick around the middle, eating too many sweet pastries."

"There're other kinds of cops." Daisy's aunt was the village safety officer. She mostly checked up on kids missing school and mediated disputes arising in the communal laundromat. Seaguard handled the most serious infractions: interclan poaching, piracy, and smuggling.

Daisy twiddled a strand of wet hair. "So what kind of cop are you?"

Morning stood and dusted her leggings. "I'd rather not talk about it."

It seemed our soak in the hot springs was over.

MORNING CAME OUT of the boathouse carrying a tackle box and a rod in a case. She laid the box open and nodded as she inspected the contents. In preparing for clients, I'd never thought to make certain the tackle box was stocked. But Morning found it acceptable and removed a container of dry flies and fishing lures.

As we returned up the trail beside the creek, Morning explained how fish liked to swim along the edges of pools at the juncture where stillness met motion. She located a spot she liked, and I sat on the bank watching. Morning, wearing a smock and leggings, stepped lightly from rock to rock, casting with skill. With grace, she sent the line arcing across the water to place a fly just so on the edge of an eddy. With a quick tug of her rod, she caught one. The fish wriggled out of the stream, sleek and wet, the line taut.

She grasped the squirming creature and brought it to me. "She's a rainbow."

"A rainbow?"

The trout lay gasping in her hands, its red gills pumping. "A kind of trout." Morning tilted the fish. "See the rainbow on her side—silver, rose, blue, and olive— spawning colors? They'll fade when she dies. I wish they could always stay this way." Morning swung the fish against a rock. It struck with a wet smack.

"You killed it," I said.

"I don't torture fish," Morning said. "I catch them—easy does it—get my data, and release them. Or I kill them immediately." She grinned.

Daisy wanted to try fishing, so Morning helped her cast, directing her arm and the lure to land in the right spot, then she helped set the hook.

"I caught one! I caught one!" shouted Daisy, her wide-set eyes huge with excitement. "What do I do?"

"Hold on!" Morning said, reaching for the line then the writhing fish.

Daisy tried to hold the wriggly, wet torpedo.

Morning grasped the fish firmly and whispered, "Oh, my darling. My lovely." She put her fingers in its mouth and pulled out the hook. "Here, kiss her." She held out the fish.

"Kiss her?" Daisy's face creased with puzzlement.

"For luck in fishing," Morning said. "You always kiss your first fish of the season."

Daisy puckered up, closed her eyes, and kissed the fish right on the mouth. "Not bad." But she grimaced.

"Tradition," Morning cooed. "The fish's soul will tell its kin of your kindness, and they'll all want to jump on our hooks." Morning whispered once more to the fish then put the creature out of its misery.

When they'd caught three fish, Morning measured and cleaned them, with each, slitting a knife from anus up the belly. She looked at the entrails. "This one is a girl. See the eggs? She was going to be a mama."

"Sad," I said.

"Sad," agreed Morning, "but tasty." She touched her ear. "Just a moment." That gesture seemed to indicate something more complex than thinking. She stood, her face animated. The fingers of her other hand flicked, showing the number three. "Okay. Done."

"What were you doing?" I asked.

Without answering, Morning closed the tackle box.

In the kitchen, Morning washed the fish and lovingly patted them dry. Then she rolled them in oatmeal and fried them in bacon grease until they were crispy and golden. She fried the milt as well but set the eggs aside in a little dish of salt and vinegar.

"Caviar," she said.

Daisy made a salad, and I fixed sandwiches for lunch. Then Daisy and I went out to the veranda, ostensibly to set the table.

"Do you think she's lying about being a cop?" I adjusted a vase of flowers. "She's so sweet. I just can't see her arresting criminals. She's kind even to fish."

"But she's fully capable of killing them," Daisy said, pouring cool mint tea. "Morning said law enforcement, not cop. That could be a number of things."

"Her only conceivable role could be as bait in a sting operation," I said, tweaking the position of a daffodil. "She could easily pass herself off as underage."

"Doesn't make sense," Daisy said. "So how does this fit with the clandestine esskip? And she sure knows her fly-fishing."

We dined on the veranda. Morning held a fish by head and tail and delicately nibbled flesh from the tiny bones. I tried to follow her example, biting gently, separating the meat from the nearly transparent skeleton.

Morning offered me the fried milt, but there wasn't even a mouthful of the substance, so she gave it to Daisy.

"What's this?" Daisy asked.

"Trout semen," Morning said.

"Fish cum! This I have to try." Daisy sampled the delicacy, puzzlement on her face as her mouth worked.

"Any good?" I asked.

"Doesn't taste like cum."

"When was the last time you tasted cum?" We always used barrier protection. I insisted on it.

"It's been a while," Daisy said. "A drawback to our work—no taste-testing the product."

We carried the dishes inside. In the kitchen, Daisy set out the drainer and filled the sink. Daisy washed the dishes, her arms immersed in frothy suds.

"When will I find out about him?" Morning asked, scraping her plate into a bucket.

"We know very little." I placed the leftover salad in the cold cupboard. "Our plan is to get you ready for whatever he and you might like, train you as our apprentice. Then when you meet him, you can make the most of your time together."

"So let's get started," Morning said, all eagerness.

Yet we still knew next to nothing about her.

# CHAPTER 04
## The Girl

DAISY LAY AGAINST the headboard, under the eaves of the cottage, her handscreen propped on her knees. A nightlight attached to the wall shone on her, the glowing disk shaded red. The prophet Catherine Smith had taught Fenrian women to use lunaception birth control. By synchronizing ovulation with the light of Luna Majora, women could predict their fertility and choose when to become pregnant. Reading after dark could scramble lunaception.

"It's late, and you'll wreck your eyes," I said. Under the covers, I stroked the swell of her hips. "Surely Lord Kopiddleko and Prissy Kotitty can break up on their own."

Daisy smiled and placed her hand over mine. "I'm trying to figure out the female pilot. Nothing. I didn't get a good look at her." She tipped her screen to show the image of a ship, not much more than a dark blob in the dim red light. "But I found this in the local news. Maybe that's where Morning came from."

She passed me the screen. The caption read: Fennako Royal Yacht sighted in Kazlofko. Morning had been photographed on a ship, but whether it was that one or another, I had no way of knowing. I skimmed the article as best I could. The FNS *Shewolf* was moored near Kazlofko Village.

"That's dozens of miles away."

"Eight dozen," Daisy supplied. "In an esskip, the distance would take less than an hour."

"They could have come from dozens of ships." I shook my head. "She and the woman pilot could have camped out, or taken lodging, or even traveled all night. Maybe they live in the area."

"But if she flew from *Shewolf*, she's associated with the Fennako Royal family."

"Maybe."

Daisy snuggled against me, her breasts pressing against mine. I adjusted a pillow under her head—her dark hair swirled over the white linen—then I propped my own head. I stroked her silken skin, her shoulders, and the length of her back.

In the morning, I went downstairs to fix breakfast. A spiral staircase led down from the loft bedrooms to the sitting room.

Morning was on the veranda and looking across the cove to the east where sunrise tinged the sky salmon pink. I threw on a wrap and joined her in dawn observances.

The two moons hung in mid-sky, both waning

quarters but not yet in phase, the little moon having nearly caught the big moon.

Morning nodded to me, and together we repeated the Noah Code in a call and response pattern.

I began, "Noah commanded, 'Observe the tide.'"

She responded, "'And you will survive.'"

Reciting the twelve precepts of the Noah Code took me back to my childhood and my great aunt teaching me proper reverence. When our ancestors had first come to Fenria, they faced conditions fiercer than those of ancient Earth. Never before had they lived with the complexity of tides driven by two moons or on a world with no continents to break the tearing winds or high seas. But we'd adapted to surviving in the grip of Poseidon.

Living on ragged archipelagos lashed by storm, we clung to reason and observation, the rule of Danna as taught by Noah. My great aunt had explained that Poseidon and Danna were the names for the polestars but were also symbols for the male and female aspects of God. Danna, the lady of justice and mercy, had been known by many names: Maria, Skadi, Metis, Athena. As the North Star, Danna stood as the still point in chaos, the rock we clung to, a woman holding aloft a torch.

The ritual words washed over me. "'Welcome the stranger. Forgive your enemies. Be prepared.'" I went within to my own still point, which is Danna. I gave the last precept. "'Educate the children of strangers.'"

Morning recited the final response, "'Teach the ways of Noah to all.'"

In the golden light of dawn, she seemed to me a young Athena. She continued with the traditional ceremony, bowing to each of the cardinal directions and greeting the moons and the rising sun as it broke, a bright sliver over the top of the purple mountains.

WE ATE BREAKFAST, toasted oats with blueberries and clabber, at the kitchen table. Morning sipped from a steaming mug. Sunlight sparkled on the cove.

"You seem to take your tidal observation seriously," I said.

She shrugged and set the cup beside her bowl.

"It's a good thing," I assured her. "Noah taught to observe the tide without. For what we're doing, we must observe the tide within just as rigorously. In order to become pregnant, you'll need to predict ovulation. Daisy and I will help, but you have the key task of following the Noah Code and tracking your cycle."

Daisy stood to clear dishes. "All twelve precepts?" she asked with a humorous glint to her eyes. "What about the seventh precept? No gossiping or boasting?"

"It's fine if you're the one gossiping or boasting. But you might want to avoid women who do."

It was believed that a woman who disregarded one precept would disregard others, including the prohibition of excessive nighttime light. Women's cycles synchronized with one another's as much as they did with the moon. The exposure of one woman to bright light could affect the ovulation of others. But only the fanatical enforced every detail of the code.

"Beware of Sappho," Daisy. said "She boasts."

"And Daisy gossips," I said. "The important thing is to sleep at regular hours." I offered Morning a pocket-sized noteboard. "You should fill this out daily." I pointed at the column for basal temperature.

"No need." Morning touched behind her ear. "I already record my temperature."

Daisy leaned against the sink.

"You'll also need to record changes in your saliva and cervical mucus," I said. "Your cycle is probably synchronized with Luna Majora, but we shouldn't make assumptions. I have a microscope to give you. May I show you how to use it and what to look for?"

Morning nodded.

The case with the equipment remained near the door. I retrieved it, set the case on the table, and opened it to display a microscope and slides. "We'll look at your saliva first." I offered her a slide. "Put a dab of spit on this. You can use your finger."

She smeared saliva it on the slide, leaving a wet streak on the glass.

"Now we let it dry," I said.

Morning gently waved the slide then set it on the table.

I reached for another slide. "We'll also observe vaginal secretions."

"Sapph, you're being too clinical." Daisy rolled her eyes. "Morning, pull down your pants so she can look at your cunt goo."

Morning shrugged and slipped down her leggings, revealing lacy panties and a triangle of pubic hair. My breath caught in my throat. Young women excite me with their innocence and the beauty of their bodies. This young woman in particular inflamed my desire. I treated all of my clients with respect, yet a ship couldn't sail without the wind or against the wind. My passion drove me, and I directed it as if close-hauled and beating into the wind.

"May I?" At her nod, I pulled on a glove and slipped my finger between her thighs, my thumb snuggled in her fur.

She gasped but held still, caught on my fingers as I teased open her labia. A thrill went through me, partly from fear that I would violate her trust. I withdrew my hand and tested the consistency of the mucus, touching thumb to forefinger.

"You've already ovulated this month," I said calmly. "During ovulation, it's the consistency of egg whites. Let's take a look under the microscope."

Morning handed me a slide, and I wiped the secretion onto the glass. She took the slide, dropped on a slide cover, and slipped the glass sandwich into place on the table of the microscope, her actions routine. She fobbed and twiddled the wheels of the scope. If I were to lift the tail of her smock, her lovely behind would be exposed, sweet buttocks, and between them her—

Morning peered into the microscope eyepiece. "What am I looking for?"

Swallowing, I maintained professional detachment. "Observe. Notice and note any changes."

Morning reached for the waist of her leggings and pulled them up. *Ah, well.* The view had been a nice idea even if I'd imagined most of it.

We used a note screen to look at photos of dried saliva. I explained how to look for fern patterns, like frost on window glass.

"This sort of observation is important, don't get me wrong," I said, "but the true thing we seek is your emotions. Daisy and I will be assisting you with the most intimate and sacred act: the conception of a child. We need to know what you want us to do."

"I don't know," Morning said.

"Then we should explore, try things out. I propose we spend the day getting comfortable with our bodies."

MORNING AND I relaxed in the sitting room, both of us wearing robes. Morning's robe was aqua-green silk, hand painted in patterns of swirling water. Daylight shone through the clerestory windows, half-rounds of glass that were much like the lunettes in the kitchen. A sliding screen divided the sitting room from the kitchen. Near the spiral stairway, we reclined on a built-in platform, a wide couch piled with bolsters and cushions.

Daisy joined us from the back, where she'd taken a shower. She wore a robe with the sash missing, her full breasts with brown areolas plainly in view. She wore her hair loose in flowing waves. Morning was staring then averted her gaze.

Daisy sat on the couch. "Go ahead. Look if you like."

"Can I touch?" Morning asked.

"That's the idea," Daisy said, draping an arm across a cushion.

Morning moved closer and, with her fingertips, stroked one of Daisy's breasts.

"Do you like?" Daisy leaned in to Morning's touch.

Morning clasped the breast with her whole hand and squeezed. Daisy giggled and slipped her robe from her shoulders, offering herself to Morning's exploration. I enjoyed watching, as if seeing Daisy's body for the first time. It was such a marvel, full breasts above a slim waist and curvaceous hips.

I moved to sit beside them. "May I have a turn?"

"Of course." Morning moved aside from Daisy.

I touched Morning's robe. "I mean with you. May I?"

She nodded and let me unwrap her. Her robe fell away from her narrow shoulders. Her body was lyrical and classically proportioned.

"Oh! You're so beautiful," I said as her breasts came into view, neither big nor small but beautifully rounded.

She recoiled.

"Too much, too fast?" I asked.

"Aye." She shut her robe.

"How about if I give you a massage? Would that be okay?"

She agreed.

Daisy adjusted a rheostat to dim the windows then turned on the sound system to the wash of water on a beach. Morning lay on the massage table. I dropped my own robe and rubbed my hands with oil. Stroking her back, I eased muscles in an honest massage. Other than my own nakedness, there was nothing sexual about it.

She was well muscled under her feminine curves. She had a hint of a suntan on her neck and arms, but it stopped at her shoulders and throat. I lost myself in the methodical movement of kneading on her arms, her feet, her legs. She had calluses at the base of her fingers. Weight lifting? Rowing? Most likely fishing. The skin of her feet was soft, no sign of forming bunions. This girl had never worn ill-fitting shoes. Slowly she relaxed under my touch, becoming pliant and yielding some of herself to me, if only her tension.

"Okay. Roll over," I said.

She obeyed, but her tension returned.

"It's all right," I said. "I won't go anywhere I'm not allowed."

I worked over her shoulders then slid my hands behind her neck, pulling, straightening her spine and easing the muscles at her nape. As I worked, my fingers brushed against bumps under her hair. I felt more carefully. Welts on her scalp?

"How about lying on your stomach again?" I said.

She rolled over, ever compliant. I smoothed her hair, examining the welts as best I could in the low lights. The scars formed a network of star patterns, evidence of a neural interface. The surgery for such implants was done in infancy, usually on boys, the child's destiny fixed as Seaguard.

"These are beautiful," I said.

"Sassafras." Morning shook off my touch. She rubbed the back of her head then sighed and relaxed. "Aye. I have a neural interface. No reason to hide it now."

I continued to massage until Morning fell asleep. I covered her with a blanket and went into the kitchen to talk with Daisy.

"She won't open up," I said. "She's nervous, but she won't say so."

Daisy perched on a kitchen stool." Sapph, give her time."

"She has a neurological implant. Same as Reolo Comryez."

"Most likely she's a medical student," Daisy said.

It was a plausible assumption. Women outside the Mediko sisterhood rarely had such implants. Surgeons used their neural interfaces to perform remote surgery.

"But what about the woman pilot?" Daisy asked.

"I'd hazard she's a surgeon," I said. Physicians weren't supposed to operate watercraft, but they did. "You saw

Morning using a microscope. She's comfortable with medical technology."

"She's worked in a lab," Daisy agreed. "But not necessarily a medical lab."

"Are you still thinking of that ship?" I asked.

"I'm thinking about how the royal family has women in the Seaguard."

"That would make Morning a princess."

"It would."

MORNING BALANCED ON a chair arm. "What next?"

"Think back to being a kid." Daisy flopped onto the cushions beside me. "Remember taking a bath with your sister."

Morning touched a finger slightly back of her ear as she did when thinking. I recognized the gesture as a habit related to implant usage. "I don't have a sister," she said. "Or a brother."

"Well, a cousin then. And drawing pictures in the soap on your cousin's back."

"Never done it."

"Then you haven't lived." Daisy jumped up. "Come on. I'll show you."

She led Morning into the bathroom and turned on a tap. Water gushed into the tub, and Daisy poured in lavender-scented bubble bath. Suds billowed into voluminous clouds, more froth than water.

Daisy turned off the tap. "Last one in is a rotten egg." She stripped, clipped her hair on top of her head, and hopped in. "I win. You're a rotten egg."

"Am not!" Morning took off her leggings and pullover, a bit more slowly than Daisy had, and stepped into the foam.

I pulled up a bench. "Mind if I stick around?"

"She's the mom." I had no desire to act as a client's mother, thank you, and Daisy stuck out her tongue. She knew what I was thinking. "Here, Morning, turn around. I'll do you."

Morning faced away, presenting her back. Daisy rubbed her hands with soap, flared her fingers like a magician, and smeared lather on Morning's back.

"Soapy sudsy. Soapy sudsy." Daisy traced a figure with her forefinger. "Now, guess what I'm drawing."

"Circle," Morning said, her damp hair dark against her neck.

"Nope," Daisy said, punctuating the figure.

"Smiley face."

"Okay, erase that," Daisy said. "What about this?"

"Heart," Morning said.

They were so innocent, so childlike in their play, yet they weren't children, not with those breasts.

"And this?" Daisy asked.

"The letter Sierra. The letter November."

Daisy frowned at me. "She's too good at this." Her finger moved again. "Read that."

Morning read the words written on her back written with only the movement of Daisy's finger. I never knew someone's back could be that sensitive.

Daisy rinsed the soap. "Now you do me."

Daisy and Morning turned around, and Morning traced figures on Daisy's violin-shaped back.

"Tell me what attracts you to a man." Daisy peered over her shoulder. "I like the muscles: nice biceps, a washboard abdomen, that sort of six-bump thing. What about you?"

"I think I like the eyes. And something here." Morning pursed her lips and touched her brow. "This part."

Daisy brightened. "You mean his mind."

"Aye. But also how he looks here." Morning stroked her eyebrow.

Daisy laughed. "Oh, you like craggy, masculine features. Sappho doesn't go for that at all. She prefers boys who resemble girls."

"I don't go for boys," I pointed out.

"Don't believe her." Daisy flicked water from her fingertips, spattering me with droplets. "How could anyone not like men?" She stood, suds slipping from her skin as if she were a nymph rising from surf. "Hey, the water's getting cold. Let's get out."

They rinsed off and let me towel them dry. I was tempted to slip that towel between Morning's legs. Daisy was better for that soap game. I'd have been too excited by Morning's body.

I tapped Daisy's shoulder. "Do you mind?"

"Can you excuse us?" she said. "We need some time alone."

We went up the stairs to the loft. Under the eaves, I shoved Daisy onto the bed and stripped.

"I couldn't stand it," I said. "She is so Poseidon-damned hot. And you're a goddess. Danna! I had to sit on my hands the whole time."

Daisy opened her legs, and I rubbed her breasts with one hand, her clitoris with the other. She gasped, losing control. I had the power.

"You're mine, you know," I said. "Nobody can do you like I can."

We turned head to tail, Daisy under me, my mouth against her. We moved together as one, equal in our passion. And then it was over, like a thunderstorm on a summer day. The pulsing slowed. *There. There. And gone.*

"Oh! That was good," Daisy said. "Do you think she heard us?"

"Probably."

Daisy and Morning sat amid the cushions in the sitting room, giggling, their heads bowed over Daisy's handscreen. Morning glanced up as I descended the staircase but didn't comment about the earlier rumpus.

I peered at the image on Daisy's screen, a close up of a man's muscular chest, his head and legs cropped. I'd never been a fan of such photography, but Daisy had a collection gleaned from old stud catalogs.

"You know we've got a larger screen," I said. "You might be able to see all of him." The main floor of the cottage had two rooms besides the kitchen, sitting room, bath, and water closet. One of the rooms was a studio, the other a bedroom. We'd set up the downstairs bedroom with a large viewing screen.

Daisy nudged Morning. "What do you think? Want these fellows even bigger?"

Morning blushed, roses blooming in her fresh skin, but she nodded.

The three of us went into the bedroom. Daisy transferred the images to the wall screen, then we piled on the bed. I surreptitiously lifted the tail of Daisy's robe to reveal her buttocks, something that interested me more than the parade of man meat.

Daisy and Morning talked over what they liked about each man and what they'd like to do with him. Daisy's enthusiasm for the subject could be infectious. They even compared photos of penises, setting up a sort of beauty pageant for male parts.

"Big looks good, but it's harder to work with," Daisy said. "It can be uncomfortable for some activities."

"How about showing her some women?" I suggested, toying with the edge of Daisy's robe.

She brought up some photos of real beauties, some svelte, sleek, and long-legged, others with marvelous curves. Morning glanced at the beauties without much interest. She casually flipped the robe back over Daisy's behind.

"If you could have your body any way you wanted, what would it be like?" Daisy asked.

"How about you?" Morning asked.

"I like my body mostly. But I'd like to be taller with longer legs. I wear high heels sometimes for an illusion of height."

"And because they make her look sexy," I said.

"And you?" Morning gave me a serious look. "Would you want to be a man?"

What I wanted was to see both of their butts naked and side-by-side. That would be a sight.

Daisy said, "Not me. I'd rather play with men than be one."

"Sometimes I see myself as a man," I said. "Not my body, but how I feel." Sexuality and gender could be complex. Desire and spirit didn't always match the body.

"It's true," Daisy said. "She's a lusty fellow."

"But I wouldn't change my body." A real penis would interfere with my work.

Morning sat up. "I'd like to be male."

"But you're attracted to men," I said. She hadn't shown much interest in women's bodies.

"Yes. And you're attracted to women," countered Morning. "Actually, I'd like to be both." She straightened her robe.

A hermaphrodite? We could work with that.

I'D SET UP lights and a camera in the studio. Facing the mirror that covered one wall, Morning opened the robe, looking at herself. Considering what? If she liked what she saw? Imagining her body as male? Holding her robe back, she cocked a hip.

"He's going to love you," Daisy said. "Show your stuff. Over here. In front of the camera."

Under the hot lights, Morning posed. Her hips swayed to one side, then she came alive, her movement fluid, simultaneously naïve and sensual, a young animal discovering the power of her own body. She dropped the robe, and it tumbled to the floor, revealing her shoulders, back, and buttocks.

"Yes. Nice. Now bend forward. Oh, he'll like this. A little farther."

She had flexibility and grace. Her legs planted wide, she bent forward and touched the ground with her fingers.

"Sway your back. Oh yes." My own depths responded with a jolt of excitement. "Nice." I wasn't kidding. "I'm getting great shots. He'll like it. Let's see more."

Morning stood.

"Turn around."

She did. A virginal goddess, apple-breasted with a slim waist and swelling hips, faced me, her face shyly averted.

"Put your hands on your thighs and thrust your hips forward," I said.

"Like this?" With a bashful smile, Morning glanced downward.

"Show off what you've got. Oh, yes!" I was in agony. "Your man is watching."

She preened her body, lithe and sleek.

"He wants to kiss you. Can you do a backbend?"

She could. She did. I came in close with my camera and moved around her, photographing the winsome details of her body: the pink tips of her breasts, the arch of her back, and the delicate petals of her labia.

"Lie down on your back with your knees up," I said.

She tried.

"That's not quite right."

"Here." Daisy dragged out a bench. "Lie on this." Morning compliant, Daisy molded her into position. "Part your lips. Not those ones. Your other ones, with your hands."

"Oh," Morning said.

I came in close, snapping shots. "He's going to like this. Open yourself to him."

The photos were excellent both as mementos and documentation of her health.

"Beautiful." I noticed that her vagina had the crescent-shaped hymen of a girl. Even without intercourse, the hymnal opening enlarges as a woman matures. "Good Danna! You're a virgin." I was surprised more by the holdover from adolescence than I was by her apparent lack of sexual experience.

Her legs shut. "Not really."

"Your hymen is intact. That's rare. Intact at two-dozen years of age. That is your correct age?"

She sat up, still under the hot lights, and crossed her arms across her breasts. "People are always thinking I'm younger than I really am."

"Might be nice." I waited for more.

"Mama says it runs in the family. A good genetic characteristic." Morning frowned.

"Longer life?" I asked.

"No." She screwed up her face. "Longer childhood. And something called neoteny. Like how dogs have been bred for domesticity with infantile characteristics. Makes Seaguard into loyal little puppies."

Both her knowledge and bitterness surprised me. Childish characteristics could be sexy in a woman—it drew me to her. The childishness which seemed to bother her conversely attracted me. A woman with a child's playfulness. Daisy was like that. Nothing sexier.

"You know those silly lap dogs with pug faces, bred to be cute?" Morning said. "That's what I am, a lap dog."

"I presume you've never engaged in sex," I said.

"That depends on what you mean by sex. Women in my family mature at a later age, so we tend to be older our first time we do it for real."

"Have you engaged in virtual sex?"

"I suppose you could call it that." She averted her eyes. "We don't talk about it much, but each Seaguard magnate perceives his territory as his own body." She rubbed her lips together. "His complete body."

I made a guess at what she'd left out. "Does this body come complete with a penis?" I supposed if there were giants in the earth, those giants would have genitalia and make love, their stony anatomy lending names to mountains and rivers.

She nodded. "Also, a lord has access to the memories of his predecessors. It's as if each magnate is the reincarnation of all who have gone before him. I haven't had sex in this body, but I remember doing it."

"I take it you're a Seaguard lord," I said. Female magnates were rare but not unheard of. Several years back, a middle-aged hospital administrator had been appointed as a Seaguard magnate and controversy had ensued.

"Sappho, I know what I'm doing," Morning said. "Many women remain physically celibate their entire lives but are quite happy. I remember."

"Still, you'll have to make a decision about your hymen. It's not a seal guaranteeing sexual purity. I can work with you to reduce the chance of tearing, or you can wait and see what happens. It could be painful and with some bleeding. Some men like that. Others don't care. So it may all be for nothing."

"I'll wait," she said with finality.

"In your memories, has there been anything particularly enjoyable?"

"Ah, well. Being a man." Her face reddened. "With another man."

"Is that what you want to do?"

"Uh-huh." She bowed her head, averting her gaze, a demure maiden who dreamed of making love as a man.

Wearing only panties, Daisy dodged behind an easy chair.

"You can't get away from the law." I strutted into the sitting room clad in a strap-on and oversized seaboots.

Earlier, Morning had expressed an interest in anal sex, so we'd accommodated her. I'd demonstrated, and we'd practiced both giving and receiving. Morning had been an eager student, and she'd quickly advanced to more complex variations. Considering Morning's perception of herself as male, this wasn't at all odd.

"Yoo-hoo, officer." Morning popped up from behind the other chair. "If you let my friend go, I'll hubba hubba." She batted her eyelashes and lifted one shoulder in a show of seduction. She played the game with enthusiasm.

"Sinking pirates!" I shouted.

Daisy yelled and ran. My feet sloshing in the boots, I pounced, and we tumbled onto the couch platform.

"I'll punish you. Punish both of you." I pulled down Daisy's panties and used my dildo on her ass.

She shrieked in mock protest.

Morning piled on top of us, her soft breasts pressing into my back. "Let her go!"

"Never!" I fell off the couch and stood. "I'll teach you a lesson."

While I replaced my condom, Daisy embraced Morning among the cushions. I applied lubricant to my dildo before carefully easing into Morning.

I dropped out of character. "Let me know if it's too much."

She took a shuddering breath. "It's good."

I withdrew.

"Do you think he'll like this?" Morning sat up.

"It only matters that you like it," I said.

"I do, but I want to be Seaguard. You be the pirate."

I laughed and removed the strap-on. I handed over the dildo, lubricant, and fresh condoms. Daisy sat beside me as I peeled off the boots. The pair of secondhand seaboots had been quite a find. Daisy had purchased them from a floating junk market aboard a barge that moved from village to village, picking up scrap and recyclables.

These seaboots had been designed for a small man, so they were sloppy around the instep but too tight in the thighs. Putting them on was a chore akin to donning tight- fitting gloves. Taking them off was nearly as difficult.

Daisy helped Morning adjust the strap-on, but Morning needed no assistance with the boots. She folded down the cuffs and pulled on one then the other with movements so smooth that she must have done it on a daily basis.

She stood, her legs planted in a wide stance, dildo angled upward. "You evil pirates. I'll get you," she intoned in a deep voice, but it cracked. She busted up laughing.

Then the game was on, Morning chasing down the pirates and meting out punishment. It was times like this when I loved my job. Daisy took a turn next. Morning helped her with the boots, and we were off. Morning scrambled up the stairway, Daisy close behind. I followed.

In our loft bedroom, Daisy shoved Morning onto the bed face down. Daisy straddled her. "You're not getting away from me, you scoundrel."

"You let me go!" Morning shouted.

I entered the room. "Daisy, be careful."

Daisy leaned to whisper in Morning's ear, "If you

mean it, use the word."

"Let me go! Right now."

My heart hammered. Morning had an implant and access to the Sense-net. Everything indicated that Daisy was manhandling a real Seaguard officer.

"I've got you right where I want you," purred Daisy. She held out her hand. "Sapph, give me the flog."

"But we haven't shown her how it works."

"Just give it to me," Daisy said.

From a case, I selected a flog of soft leather strips braided around a handle.

Daisy took it and rubbed the leather against Morning's back. "This might sting, but that's all. It's like birch twigs in a sauna. Are you okay with this?"

"Aye. Permission given." Morning spoke clearly, her wording almost mechanical.

"You evil thing. Do you think your man's going to like what you've been doing? Messing around with someone else? Take that." Daisy sent the flog down in a cascade of leather that splashed across Morning's back. "You belong to one man. No one else." Daisy brought down the flog again.

"I'll never do it again." Morning made a show of apologizing.

The flog descended again, and as if an electric shock went through Morning's body, she jerked and writhed. Daisy stroked between Morning's legs. She arched and spasmed then went limp.

Morning sat up and grinned. "That was fun." Then her expression became serious. "Do you think there's something wrong with me? I must want to be punished."

"There's nothing wrong with you," I said. "This is pretend."

"My feelings aren't," she said. "It's not fair. I'll get to meet with him once. Only once in person and then never again." She fiddled with her sash.

**CHAPTER 06**
**Comryez**

OUR CASES AND duffles remained on the office floor. Daisy and I had returned home after three enjoyable days with Morning. Daisy had been disappointed when a man, not the mysterious female pilot, arrived with the esskip to transport Morning.

The dame hailed, her name announced by speakers in my planning screen. Daisy and I were in the process of unpacking, cleaning, and sorting equipment and supplies. Daisy stepped over a duffle and sat on the arm of the sofa. I sat at my desk, and we exchanged greetings.

"My niece is pleased," the dame said. Her hair seemed to have been recently dyed, the gray no longer showing. "I have more information on the man. I believe you'll find it helpful with this project." A page of text replaced her image as she signed off.

Daisy leaned forward. "That looks like genetic records."

"Aye." This would be much more useful than the legal documents we'd previously received. The packet also appeared to contain health records.

Daisy transferred the data to her handscreen. "Oh?" She flicked pages.

I sat beside her on the sofa. "What are you oohing and aahing about?"

Daisy looked up, a finger on her screen. "The man *is* Reolo Comryez, the son of Stink Lily, but not by Teakh Noahee."

"So Stink Lily didn't sneak into the cell of Outlaw Teakh and steal his semen? Wasn't that the rumor?" It was the sort of juicy gossip Daisy adored.

"This is even better," Daisy said. "His full name is Reolo Noahee Comryez. He's the only known descendant of Teakh Noahee. Teakh's grandson. His grandmother was Stellamara Matlawko Mara. That's where the Littlemara name came from."

"Surely there's more than one. I recall he had nine boys."

"Reolo Comryez is the only one we know about for sure. I'd say the liaison is a match made by eugenicists. Here's another interesting tidbit. On his mother's side, Reolo has multiple generations of inbreeding. Comryez engage in sexual relations with members of their own clan. Judging by genealogy, the Comryez celibacy requirement is a cover for incest."

"So why aren't they freaks?" I asked.

"Because it's carefully done. They're breeding for specific characteristics. One of the characteristics is— get this—neoteny, childish characteristics retained into adulthood."

"You mean like Morning?"

"The eugenicists are after neurological flexibility. Both Morning and this guy retain childhood neurons for a longer period of time, so they learn quickly. Delayed puberty is a side effect. This family tree also has Teakh's mother, but not the name of Teakh's father or his multiple wives."

"What about Reolo's health and sexual preferences?" I asked.

"He has a male lover." Daisy grinned. "But his records show him as heterosexual."

"Bisexual, just like you, my dear." I squeezed Daisy's shoulder. "What does his lover think about this?"

"He's the source of this information and seems to be partly responsible for setting up this liaison. He's older than Reolo and married with children, but he doesn't give his name or clan." Daisy bent and continued reading. "A photo!"

She turned her screen to show me Reolo Comryez standing calf-deep in water with dark, wet rocks behind him. Given the angle of the shot, the photographer was either in the water or on a boat. He wore nothing more than a life vest and seaboots. On his erect penis, the glans pushed past the foreskin, the tip jet black.

I stepped back from the bizarre image. "I've never seen anything like that."

"I've seen that coloration occasionally," Daisy said. "Quite sexy on a nicely shaped penis such as his."

"So what do you have on his health?"

Daisy flipped pages. "This has only partial medical records, but both the lover and his wife test clean." Daisy gave a sly grin. "Maybe the wife is pushing for this liaison, trying to get her husband back."

"What about Reolo? What does he get out of being with Morning?"

"I'd hazard he's after a more appropriate partner. According to his records, he prefers women."

"But this is a one-time liaison."

"Once is better than never," Daisy said. "The two men engage in elaborate sex play in the Comryez Narrows. It's a strait with a massive tidal bore, two-dozen meters of head flooding through a narrow passage twice a day. That's a lot of water with tremendous power."

"A giant geographic dick." Now there was a detail to impress Daisy. "Best get out of the way."

"Sex in front of a tidal wave. They make out as the bore tide is approaching. Reolo likes his lover to rough him up. Rape scenarios."

I sobered. That wasn't a joking matter but dangerous for everyone involved.

Daisy waved her handscreen. "According to this, it's consensual."

"Do we want Morning in the middle of this?" I asked.

"It's not our choice. It's theirs. And they might be a good match, both into submission and dominance."

"Except they're both submissive. One of them will have to take charge, or one of us will."

Daisy shook her head. "I'm not very good at dominance."

"You did quite well the other day." I recalled how she'd flogged and berated Morning, a reversal of our usual roles. When a customer requested domination, I usually became the dominatrix.

"I don't look the part," Daisy said, "and it'll be different with a man. How about you? Are you ready to act as dominatrix to a man who plays chicken with a tidal wave?"

"Maybe Morning will come through as our dominant."

"The girl has steel in her," Daisy said. "Don't let her sweetness throw you off. You saw her with those fish and how she took the hooks out."

"This isn't about just conceiving a child, though," I said. Neither Morning nor Reolo had demonstrated a strong interest in becoming parents, and that concerned me.

DAISY AND I waited at the dock, the sun still below the horizon and the night sky yielding to pearly gray. We'd returned to Cozy Cove for another monthly rendezvous with Morning. This time we had a better understanding of what she was up against, and I wondered how much she knew of the situation with Reolo. Her interest in anal sex suggested she had some idea of what he was dealing with and of how to help him.

In my pocket, I carried condoms, lubricant, and gloves. I followed the third precept of Noah: be prepared.

Daisy pushed back her hood, and her hair billowed in the wind. "Do you think Morning will arrive with the female pilot? I still want to get a good look at that woman."

The gray esskip taxied toward us in the shell-pink dawn. The canopy opened to reveal only one person aboard—Morning. She'd flown the craft herself.

She smiled and waved. As the esskip glided toward the dock, she secured bumpers against the hull. "Can you give me a hand?"

She tossed me a mooring line, and I secured it to a cleat. I did know how to tie a clove hitch. Morning passed a duffle to Daisy then a larger bag to me. Morning stepped onto the dock wearing seaboots. Hers were gray-green and fit perfectly, the articulation of the knees molded perfectly to her legs. They must have been custom made. She also wore a gray-green life vest. Both boots and vest lacked ornamentation.

Morning tied off her craft with additional lines and checked that the cockpit was clean.

"Her kit," Daisy whispered. "No decoration. Extremely high status." Daisy, who notices such things, had told me that people who are confident of their status dress down. To the unobservant, these people appear to be unimportant, but details of quality give them away, details such as fit and lack of pattern on a color that was likely to show stains and scuff marks.

"Understated," I said.

"Those boots scream quality and understatement."

I raised my eyebrows. Commenting would be rude since Morning had chosen not to share her identity.

Seemingly satisfied with the condition of her craft, Morning stepped out, and the canopy closed behind her. Morning gave one of her shy grins. "I want to try some things out."

We went up to the house. In the sitting room, Morning opened the bag. She rummaged inside and brought out a skin-toned object. "I brought this." The device dangled from her hand, her own strap-on dildo. "It works with my neural interface, a telechiric."

Oh, Lord Poseidon! What happened to our reticent Seaguard girl?

# CHAPTER 07
## Hermaphrodite

I INSPECTED THE device, a high-quality phallus. Similar to the ones used for insemination, it had a reservoir for either semen or artificial cum. The color of the tool was an exact match to Morning's medium skin tone, surely custom made like her boots.

"Remote control." She nodded enthusiastically. "Works in conjunction with my neuro, so I can feel it like it's the real thing."

Daisy met my glance. It seemed our girl, technically still a virgin, had been doing research.

Morning tapped behind her ear. "I've got the manual on my neuro."

"Oh. That looks like fun. Can I see?" Daisy held out her hands, and I gave her the device. She wobbled the artificial penis. "It's slack."

"The manual says it erects in response to thought," Morning said. "That is, if I get excited. Do you think I got the size right? I had it custom made."

"Try it on," Daisy said. "I want to see."

Morning pulled down the top of her leggings, exposing her buttocks and pubis, the hair much shorter than it had been before.

Daisy helped her. "Does that feel right? Maybe a little tighter here." Daisy tugged a strap.

"It can be hooked up for peeing too." Morning lifted her new penis. "It's great for taking a leak over the side of a boat."

"Looks great," Daisy said. "But not with the leggings."

"I'll have to take off my boots," Morning said.

"So put them back on."

Morning sat on the wide couch and removed the boots and leggings, then she put her feet back into the boots and adjusted the tops around her thighs. The tail of her shirt fell and covered the device.

"No testes?" I said.

"No fake veins either," Morning said. "It's supposed to work as a penis, not to look like one."

"Nothing fake about that." I reached toward her shirttail but didn't touch. The strap-on had the look of Seaguard equipment, functional and high quality, nothing imitation or purely for show.

"Except for the color," Morning said. "I thought maybe bright purple, but it didn't look right."

"The shirt hangs down too far," Daisy said. "Wear the life vest."

Morning unfastened the vest and set it aside then peeled off her shirt and chemise. She put the vest back on and fastened it. She stood wearing only the penis and a Seaguard life vest. "What do you think?"

"The size suits you, and the color is perfect," Daisy said.

In Seaguard kit, she was hot. Oh, yes, seeing her, I

understood the appeal of a lover in uniform.

"Unfasten the life vest," Daisy said. "Arch a little bit."

"Holy Poseidon!" Desire rushed into my labia, majora and minora.

Morning smiled shyly, both male and female, the combination of status and understatement stunning.

I couldn't keep my hands off her. "Here, put your leg up." I donned gloves and offered her a chair.

She put her foot on the seat, and I reached under her cock, feeling for the clitoris and labia behind it.

"Oh, no, you don't" Daisy said. "We've got to take pictures." We'd again set up a downstairs room as a photo studio.

Morning put her foot down. I straightened and removed my gloves.

"Her man's going to love this," Daisy said.

"But with these green boots and vest, her clan is obvious. He'll know who she is." She was, without a doubt, Fennako Seaguard and very likely a member of the royal family.

"Let's worry about that later," Daisy said, going ahead into the studio.

"Then you know who I am?" Morning asked.

"We know who your clan is. That color is difficult to miss." I indicated her boots.

"But it's not a bright color," Morning said.

"No ignoring what it means." The subtlety of the gray-green boots could only mean Fennako royal family, but if so, why hadn't Daisy found Morning in the scandal sheets?

"I want to dress like this for him," Morning said.

"Don't worry." I arranged three director's chairs. "We'll get it figured out." But I didn't know how. I'd intended to conceal Morning's neuro, but her Seaguard kit—real Seaguard kit—and telechiric penis shredded those plans.

Morning strutted, showing off her new equipment, and Daisy operated the camera.

"I'd like to see it erect," Daisy said.

"I'm trying, but it's not working." Morning's face creased.

"Maybe read the manual," I suggested. "Do you have it in your bag?"

"It's on my neuro." Morning set her finger behind her ear, pointing to her implant. "I'll transfer it."

Daisy sat, unfolded her screen, and read. "I don't understand. Morning, you'd better read it."

Morning sat, one hand on her new equipment, and closed her eyes, apparently reading. I glanced toward Daisy, who shrugged.

"Okay. I got it," Morning said. "My penis duplexes to the part of my brain that handles my clitoris. My brain is supposed to interpret sensation from the device as coming from my body, but I have to program my brain first."

Daisy scratched her head. "That sounds uncomfortable."

"It's not," Morning said. "It's sort of like learning to walk or to skip. To learn the connection, my brain must feel the same sensation coming from both places."

Daisy shook her head. "And this means?"

"First, I have to shave again," Morning said. "I'm not getting good contact. Then I need some jelly. And plenty of practice."

MORNING TOOK A shower, then I directed her to sit on the massage table with a towel and sheeting under her hips. Daisy propped her up with pillows, and Morning leaned back.

I calmed myself. Shaving required a steady hand. I pulled on new barrier gloves. She was something precious, something not to be sullied. She opened her legs, presenting herself to me, trusting me. With Daisy watching, I lathered Morning, enjoying the soap over her skin and the excuse to touch her, then went to work easing away hair, revealing the smooth beauty beneath. I took my time enjoying the feeling of power, as if I were sculpting her from soapstone.

Morning relaxed. I used a warm cloth to wipe away lather and began again. She became baby smooth. I cupped my hand over her mound—couldn't help myself—then stooped, sealing my work with a light kiss.

"Feels good, yes?" Daisy said, peering at my handiwork. "I told you so."

Morning sat up, rubbed her legs together, and smiled.

"But it feels best if one person has hair," Daisy said with a shake of her shoulders. "The man."

I much preferred the delightful smoothness between Daisy's legs.

"Do you think he has hair? Do you think he shaves?" Morning asked.

"Well…" I recalled the photo of Reolo. "He shaves his face. But not the part you're concerned about."

"Then you've seen him?"

"I've seen a photo. I'm sorry, I shouldn't have mentioned it."

"What does he look like?"

"Very handsome," I said. "You'll have to wait."

Daisy touched her heart then waved a hand before her exhaled breath. "Gorgeous. Really gorgeous."

"Daisy, you're raising her expectations. She'll be disappointed."

"Not with this man," Daisy said.

Morning grabbed her harness. "Let's practice."

While I cleaned up, Morning again dressed in boots and vest, and we returned to the photo studio. Try as she might, Morning still couldn't get a reaction from her device. So Daisy had her sit on a bench and, looking extremely pleased, knelt.

"Sassafras," I said. "Morning, how do you sterilize that thing?"

"I don't know," she said.

"Better use one of these." I passed Daisy a condom.

"I can't put it on her," Daisy said. "She's not erect."

I reached into my pocket for a female condom. "Try this."

Daisy, holding the barrier in place, slid her mouth over Morning's penis. They both tried, and Daisy was good, but with no success.

I strapped on my own harness, pulled a condom in place, and anointed it with lubricant. "Okay. Get off her." I pushed Daisy away and shoved Morning to her knees. "You kneel. Right now!" I slid my equipment into her butt. "Daisy, help me out."

Daisy licked Morning's cock then took it in her mouth.

"Your man will be so angry with you when he finds out what you've been doing. He's going to... He's going to..." I struggled for ideas.

Daisy matched my rhythm, and Morning doubled over.

"I'm going to hurt you." I blustered, attempting to play the role of dominatrix. "You'll hurt all over when I'm through with you."

"It's working," whispered Morning. "Keep going."

"Your man is going to tie you up and punish you."

"Got it!" Morning said.

I withdrew, and Daisy backed off. All three of us were panting. Morning's hair stuck to her forehead, slick with sweat, but she was beaming, penis proudly erect.

"Quick! Get the camera," I said.

Morning pulled off the condom then posed, showing off. Daisy snapped photos. Oddly, the results resembled the images of Reolo in his Seaguard boots and vest with an erect penis.

But her erection didn't last long.

Morning arrived for breakfast, her robe open and her penis hanging slack. "The manual says to practice by wearing it." She touched behind her ear. "And there're exercises in here."

Daisy sat at the table. "Let's see." She opened her handscreen and read, a finger to her lip. "We can do this."

"What?" I asked.

Daisy read from the manual. "'For training, both clitoris and penis are stimulated at the same time, establishing parallel sensation.'"

"It says not to do it all at once," Morning said. "Little sessions. I've set up a schedule."

"A schedule?" Oh yes, Morning was taking charge.

"The schedule should produce the optimum effect in the shortest amount of time," Morning said solemnly. "That's also why I'm not wearing panties. More stimulation if it's exposed. We're altering neurons in my brain. Repetition initiates the process, but my brain makes the actual changes during sleep."

"Let me see that." I reached for Daisy's handscreen.

Morning gulped her breakfast while I looked over the exercises. For most of them, stimulation done by another person was recommended, although some involved self-stimulation.

"This says no condom use while doing the training exercises," I said.

"Reduces stimulation," Morning explained. "Says, if necessary, use a similar material over the clitoris."

I scrolled through the instructions. "'Once the initial training is completed, condom use is fine and even recommended for multiple partners. Sterilization procedures reduce the life of the device.'"

I considered the risks. Daisy and I would be stimulating Morning with both our hands and our mouths. All three of us had recently received medical checkups in preparation for the rendezvous, and the contact would be primarily between mouth and telechiric.

I said, "For the initial phase, I'm comfortable going without barrier protection. Daisy, what about you?"

"That thing is spanking new. No problem. Let's start." Morning grinned.

After breakfast, we laid a velvet coverlet over the bed in one of the downstairs rooms. Morning set aside her robe, and we helped her get comfortable with bolsters propping up her hips. That gave Daisy and me room to work, displaying the delicate lips of her vagina, all vulnerable and pink, and above it, her slim penis.

I dimmed the lights and turned on soft music programmed to end when the exercise was done. The manual had recommended music to assist with neurological coordination. Daisy wetted her finger with lubricant and slid it under the harness, reaching for Morning's clitoris. At the same time, she took the phallus in her mouth.

I touched Daisy's shoulder. "Mind taking your clothes off?"

"Not at all. Excuse me, Morning." Daisy undressed then continued.

I sat in a chair, my palm on my own mons, enjoying the shifting of Daisy's back, head, and shoulders. Morning's gentle sighs and moans melded with the flute music. Too soon, the music ended.

"Oh, that was nice." Morning sat up, snugged her harness, and slipped on her robe, still unbelted.

Daisy put on a robe as well. We went into the sitting room.

I sat amidst the cushions. "How long will this phase take?"

"I'm not sure." Morning, wrapped in aqua silk, relaxed beside me. "I'd like to get to phase two tomorrow."

Daisy sat on a chair. "Is that realistic?"

"I'm a quick learner with these things," Morning said. "I'll show you how telechirics work." Her fingers brushed my hand. "I'm touching you. Yes?"

I agreed.

"But that's an illusion." She took my hand, her grasp firm. "This hand only seems to be yours. Your brain sends a message, and this hand responds. You're tricked into thinking this hand is yours. As long as sensation is coordinated, the illusion is maintained." She released my hand.

I inspected my hand, rotating my wrist, noticing how it moved in response to my commands and how I felt it moving. Wrist, hand, and fingers perfectly obeyed my thoughts.

Morning said, "The thing you feel with is your hand,

no matter what it actually is. Even if it's on the other side of the planet, it's still yours. I have many hands, and I'm good at adapting to new ones. So moving to phase two tomorrow just might be realistic."

I inspected my hands, imagining them operating miles away, maybe in the distant Andean Ocean, as if I could reach out and touch anything on the planet. "So where are you? Where are your hands right now?"

Morning leaned against a cushion. "We aren't supposed to talk about it with non-Seaguard. But I can tell you that I'm aware of my esskip down by the dock. My wings are behind my back, and I'm floating on the water. Can you tell me what your second toe on the right foot is doing at the moment?"

I laughed. "I've a practical consideration. We need condoms for phase two. I didn't bring enough." Once the initial neuro pathways were established, we'd use condoms.

# CHAPTER 08
## Condoms

STANDING NEAR THE spiral stairway, I tapped my com-unit and hailed the pharmacy in the nearest village. "I'm in need of a case of condoms."

"We've got them available. What kind do you need?"

"Sanitary condoms."

"We've got prophylactic condoms, gender selection condoms, and female condoms."

"Sanitary condoms."

"Are you sure? Always good to have some spermicide, in case. You never know."

"Just sanitary." I didn't want to chance getting spermicide in the wrong place.

"Sorry, fresh out."

Daisy, listening in on the conversation, grimaced.

I tried another village. The pharmacy had them in stock, but we'd have to arrange for delivery. I contacted a water taxi. They wouldn't be able to get the condoms to us until the next day.

"I'll take care of this." Morning put a hand to her ear

then smiled and nodded, clearly in communication with someone. "It'll be here in about a half hour."

"What did you do?" Daisy said.

"Made a request to the local Seaguard," Morning said. "Under the code of hospitality."

"Is that legitimate?" Daisy asked. "Could I hail and ask for deliveries?"

"The need must be clear," Morning said. "The local magnate knows I'm here under hospitality, and he knows what this place is used for. Our need is related to the Sense-net, integrating a telechiric device. Completely legitimate. He asked about the fishing. Nice guy."

MORNING LAY ON the bed, her hips propped on a bolster. I never could have been a full-time gynecologist. I couldn't have maintained professional detachment.

I wetted my finger with lubricant and slid it under the harness, feeling the faint prickle of stubble as I reached for her clitoris. I slid my mouth over her penis and strove to keep movement coordinated, sensation identical. But good Danna, it was difficult. Below my chin was one of the most beautiful pussies I'd ever seen, almost as nice as Daisy's, but virginal and off-limits. Morning had made it clear that she wanted no vaginal penetration. I longed to explore the valleys between her labia and thighs. But I had a job to do: suck on the cock.

"Delivery on its way," Morning said, still accepting my ministrations.

I kissed the base of her penis, nearly on her delectable pussy. The music ended, and I helped her sit up.

"Thank you." She put on her robe.

I went to the dock alone. A red-and-white esskip, the colors of the local clan, sped into sight. It splashed down, folded its wings, and came toward me. Bumping the dock, the canopy opened. A young man stood, fresh-faced and eager.

"What are you about?" I said.

"Observing the tide. And got a delivery."

"Thank you."

He caught sight of the gray esskip lashed to the dock. "Where'd you get her? Never seen an esskip like that before."

"Me neither," I said honestly.

He reached into the cockpit for the package. "Interesting supplies."

I smiled.

"Do you need any help?"

"We'll be all right."

"Are you sure?" He smiled, as eager as a puppy. "Always ready to offer hospitality."

Daisy might have taken him up on that, but not me. "Your offer is appreciated." I bowed. "Honor is yours."

Crestfallen, he gave up the package. "I'll be on my way."

"You do that. Tide carry you."

"Tide carry." The canopy closed, and he scooted away in his esskip then tipped a wing to me as he flew off.

DAISY MET ME on the veranda. A cool breeze trembled the leaves of the old birch tree.

"I need to talk with you," she said.

I set the condoms near the door, then we turned and walked toward the boathouse.

"Do you still think she's being exploited?" Daisy asked.

"She flies her own esskip, and she can call for help at any time. No. The man on the other hand..."

"Aye," Daisy said, our feet crunching on the gravel pathway. "I've been puzzling out the lover. I believe he's Lord Komoko. Let me show you what's happening." She snapped open the frame of her handscreen. "Here's a map of Comryez Pass. You can see it's funnel-shaped. When the tide rises in the north—that's the wide end at the top—it comes in as a wave. The shape of the pass restricts the wave, increasing the speed and power until it expends itself on the other side, which is Komoko Sound. See to the south? Remember what Morning told us about the Sense-net. Seaguard magnates feel the tide as if it moves through their bodies."

"The lovemaking of giants," I said.

"Aye. The Narrows acts as a geographic telechiric, like Morning's little pal but bigger. Way bigger."

I estimated the length of the geographic penis to be three-dozen miles. "Poseidon-damn! Reolo has the biggest cock on the planet."

"And he's fucking Komoko Sound," Daisy said. "Lord Komoko is the recipient whether he likes it or not."

"What about Reolo?" I said. He couldn't stop the tide any more than Komoko could.

"Neither of them has a choice. That's why I'm worried about him," Daisy said. "About the rape scenarios. I'm thinking they're not fantasies but scheduled exercises, like what we're doing with Morning. The men are trying to gain control of a giant-sized telechiric. Reolo's own clan did this to him. Bred him for it even. He had no choice."

"Wait a moment." I paused beside the boathouse. "Isn't that in a sense what every mother does: produce a child and stick it with a body, male or female? And with uncontrollable urges? Doesn't matter what the child wants."

"But the body and urges come out of the child's nature, not from a clan's decision. I'm not so sure about Morning." Daisy kicked at a stone. "That she's not being exploited in a similar manner."

"Oh, come on." I gestured toward Morning's gray esskip floating near the end of the dock, proof the girl could travel as she pleased.

"Listen, Sapph, I've been doing more research, trying to figure out Morning's profession. Bear with me. You know the studs we work with, they all have other jobs. It's not a full-time career."

"What about that one client of yours? The one who wouldn't go away?"

"He wasn't selling, just wanted sex. So I cut him off. No market for his splat."

"Right." He'd been creepy. If Daisy and I had wanted to be prostitutes, we wouldn't have needed medical training. Sex should be meaningful and enjoyable for everyone involved, never purely a business transaction.

"The really expensive studs are Seaguard," Daisy said. "The top studs are so expensive, they don't get much demand, not through normal channels anyway. Their other work must be safe and compatible with their use as studs. Get this—the most common job for top studs is fly-fishing."

"Truly?"

"They use smart hooks, ones that test for trout DNA." Daisy touched the boathouse door. "Then they send the guy off to remote streams—he flies his esskip there—and he reports data. Doesn't matter all that much if the data is useful. The guy comes back after doing a lot of outdoor activity, and he looks good."

"Morning claimed to be a cop." I shook my head. "In law enforcement anyway."

"So was Teakh Noahee."

"No." I couldn't quite see Morning as a female Teakh Noahee. Yet if she frequently worked undercover, Fennako would have good reason to keep photos of her private and not available to the scandal sheets.

"He did that type of fly-fishing." Daisy inclined her head toward the boathouse and the unseen tackle box shelved within. "He also worked in sting operations against poachers. In some circles, he's better known as a fisheries detective than as a stud. That was before he went rogue, kidnapped his children, and started blackmailing the poachers. Imagine Morning in a sting operation. Poachers wouldn't know what hit them."

She did have a clandestine esskip, and her pictures didn't appear in the scandal sheets.

"Will she go rogue?" I asked.

"That's the question."

# CHAPTER 09
## Hide and Seek

ON THE THIRD and final day of the session, we went out on the grounds and played hide-and-seek, each of us armed with a strap-on and a pocketful of condoms. Whoever saw the other person first got to do the honors. Morning went for the anal version and would accept a blow job but only if caught. Daisy liked to get caught, which made Morning much more interesting as prey.

Giving a blow job to a woman packing a functional penis turned me on like nothing else. Her device had an extremely short refractory period, so she could be ready for more almost immediately. But I was fair and went after both of them equally. What a marvelous day: sneaking through the woods to push a squealing girl onto the ground and drive into her, only to be jumped by another girl and her strap-on pal.

That night we all slept together under the eaves, happy and tired.

"I didn't get to do half of what I wanted," Morning said while packing up. "I brought all this stuff for nothing."

She put a fishing rod, more boots, clothing, and flogs into her bag.

"But you were prepared," I said. "You didn't know for sure what would happen."

"I suppose so."

At breakfast, Morning was fully dressed in leggings and smock, but she had a telltale bulge in her lap. She pulled on her boots and life vest. Daisy and I helped her carry her baggage to the dock. As we approached, the gray esskip twitched, and the canopy opened. Morning stooped to untie a line.

"So," I said, gesturing to the craft, "this esskip works like your little pal."

"Sure does," Morning said. "My bigger pal. Here's my arm." A wing moved. "And my finger." A pinion plate twitched.

"What about the cock?" Daisy asked.

"Daisy!" I exclaimed.

"Doesn't have one." Morning grinned. "Splashing down would be too much fun." She raised her eyebrows. "Touch and go?"

I laughed at the new type of masturbation, Seaguard practicing circuit landings.

"Too bad," Daisy said. "So tell me, you've been tied up to the dock this whole time?"

Morning grinned.

"Kinky," Daisy said.

Laughing, Morning slung her bags into the back and secured them. Then we said our good-byes. She and Daisy kissed.

As they finished, Daisy gave that bulge a squeeze. "See you later, pal."

Morning stooped to untie the last line, and I almost goosed her, but I restrained myself. Coiling the line, she stepped into the craft, her momentum carrying the craft away. She sat, and the canopy closed, hiding her behind its smoked glass. She flew away, a graceful gray dove winging over the ocean.

Daisy and I packed up. At noon, our water taxi arrived. We arrived home late and too tired to do anything besides sleep. The next day we went about unpacking, sorting, and cleaning.

Then the dame hailed. Her pinched face came up on my planning screen. "Tell us. Will our niece be ready for her duty?"

That depended on what was meant by duty.

"She's well prepared and eager to meet her man," I said.

"He is not her man. Only the assigned father of her child."

"Yes." I didn't contradict the hag. I truly thought of her as a hagfish, the sinking, parasitic eel.

"Well then. We have a tentative date for their ah... little meeting. One day. He arrives at sunrise and leaves by sunset."

"A day! Only a day?" Daisy said, leaning against my desk.

"Ma'am," I said, "we need more time."

"What for? It's a simple procedure."

"The man and your niece have never met." I wasn't entirely sure of that, but I believed they'd never met in person. "They need time to become accustomed to each other."

"They should not become accustomed to each other."

"Consider," I said. "Among other things, your niece

might not ovulate at that time. Giving them more time increases the chance that she will become pregnant."

"If I had my way, she wouldn't become pregnant. One day only. Sunrise to sunset."

The screen blinked off.

Sinking depths! I shoved back from my desk and stood. "Poseidon-damn it all!"

## CHAPTER 10
## Rendezvous

THE GRAY ESSKIP flew toward us and lightly touched down on the bay. I recognized the girl by the grace of her flight and the way she approached the dock, kissing it with her wingtip without bumping.

Daisy and I had arrived at Cozy Cove a day early to prepare it for our clients—both of them this time. Knowing that Morning liked fishing, we checked the creek and woods for trash. We actually found some of our own condoms. Whoops!

But when the smoked canopy drew back, she was not alone. A woman stood from the passenger seat and handed off a line. Her mouth, under her huge glasses, was somber, unsmiling. I fastened line, and the woman passed us the baggage, including a tackle box and case for a fly rod.

She bowed to Daisy and me. Morning stepped out, and the woman moved to the pilot seat.

"Love you," the pilot said. "It'll be okay."

Morning smiled. "Love you too."

The smoked glass canopy closed, and the esskip flew back the way it came.

IN THE KITCHEN, we planned Morning's first encounter with her man. I thought it would be lovely for them to meet on the creek, Morning naked and holding her fly rod.

She grimaced. "Biting gnats. They adore me."

"Maybe in the house," I said.

"I want…" She closed her eyes and put her hand to her ear. "We want… naked. In the house. Tied up."

"Wow!" Daisy said. "Fully naked? What about your hip-boots?"

"No boots," Morning said.

"And your little pal?" Daisy said.

Morning's face compressed. "I don't know. Do you think he'll like it?"

"Well," I said, "what are you trying to show him? You are communicating by how you meet him. What is your message?"

"That I want him. I want him to want me."

"To give yourself to him completely?" I said. "For him to do as he pleases with you?"

Morning nodded. "That's it."

I touched my fingertips together. "I recommend showing yourself completely naked and vulnerable. Leave off your little pal, at first anyway."

In the end, we chose the simplest of options: the downstairs bedroom with Morning displayed on the bed. We arranged the room, moving furniture. Daisy collapsed the wall screen and stowed it. I checked the sound system and made sure the room was stocked with lubricant, tissues, and condoms.

Then Daisy didn't like the color of the bedspread. We tried out every color available, putting samples of clothing beside Morning's skin to judge the effect. Daisy announced that we had to order a new bedspread. This time we paid for delivery. The need for condoms could be considered an emergency. The need for a color that appropriately complemented a woman's skin tone was not.

Daisy and I had found out what we could, but the man could be a monster. Given the colossal size of his geographic cock, he was a monster. I prayed that Morning's defenselessness would give him pause. Danna help her. If the man failed to be kind and gentle, she was inviting abuse.

On the morning of his arrival, I lay Morning on the massage table and shaved her, then checked between her legs for smoothness. She sat up.

"Daisy and I will meet him on the dock," I said. "We must talk with him. You stay in the house, and don't peek. You each should wear one of these." I handed her a hood, blue and richly embroidered with gold thread. "Put it on."

She did. It covered her head and the upper part of her face, long enough in the back to cover her neuro scars but open in the front.

"Does it block your vision at all?" I asked.

She turned her head and pinched the bridge of the nose where it fit snugly. "It's fine."

"I'm still not sure blue is right for you," Daisy said. "But you can't use gray-green."

Reolo hailed. His voice came over my com-unit, announcing his imminent arrival.

"Is that him?" Morning asked.

"Yes."

We left her pacing in the sitting room as Daisy and I walked to the dock.

A black esskip sped into the cove and splashed down. The high tail bore a strip of black fabric over the call numbers, but the craft had the markings of a killer whale: white eyespots and underbelly. The wings folded against the fuselage as the craft glided toward us.

"Clan Komoko," Daisy said. "Orca totem."

The canopy retracted to reveal two men. One of them, not the pilot, stood as the esskip drew near. He was dressed all in black: shirt, vest, pants, and seaboots.

Carrying a mooring line, he lightly stepped from wing-shoulder to dock. He wore his hair in black braids done up in tight rows, the ends wrapped in gold wire. The back of his head, freshly shaved and oiled, displayed the intricate welts of a Seaguard neuro. His knife attached over his heart gleamed, onyx inlaid with gold. Such custom-designed clothing must have been months in the making. He'd dressed as a bridegroom but without any indication of clan. On his left wrist he wore a silver bracelet depicting gulls in flight. The workmanship was in an older style, and black tarnish filled the grooves delineating wings and beaks. A family heirloom?

He secured the line then bowed. "Greetings."

The pilot stepped ashore next. His Seaguard kit matched Reolo's. Traditionally a bodyguard accompanied a bridegroom as the groom's witness. For an arranged marriage or expensive studs, this trusted companion witnessed the act to ensure terms of the contact were fulfilled. In the past, sperm had been stolen and sold on the black market.

Given his impressive size and the markings of the esskip, Reolo's witness was none other than Lord Antares Komoko, Reolo's friend and lover. Lord Komoko projected authority. It wasn't just his size, but the way he carried himself, a looming calmness like a dark thunderhead. He wasn't a man to be messed with. We bowed. They bowed.

"What are you about?" I asked the traditional question.

"We honor the tide." Komoko's voice boomed deep with words more formal than the usual response.

I gulped and swallowed. "I am Sappho, and this is my partner, Daisy."

"I'm Reolo, and this is—"

I stopped him. "We know. But this is supposed to be anonymous. I recommend you use a nickname."

"Well, some people call me Blackmouth." He stuck out his tongue, showing off the velvety black color. "And some people call me Pirate."

Komoko ruffled Reolo's braided hair. "Pipsqueak."

"Maybe think about it," I said. "We need to come to an agreement on guidelines for behavior. Shall we talk about this in private?" I nodded toward Komoko.

"He stays," Reolo said. "He's looking out for me."

"Aye. Your witness," I said.

"Let it be understood you are here to father a child with a woman you do not know. You both will remain anonymous. Agreed?" I'd given a similar talk to Morning.

"Aye." Reolo smiled, an expression which lit his whole face, his eyes sparkling, his teeth bright white. Just as quickly, the smile was gone.

"Please understand there is nothing you're required to do," I said. "You do not have to father this child, and you are free to leave at any time. The young woman has chosen to go by the name Morning. I ask that you treat Morning, Daisy, and me with respect. We will give you the same respect. Morning has a safeword, *sassafras*. She will say this if there's something she doesn't want done to her. Be forewarned she likes to playact, and she has some interesting tastes. I think you'll get along. I recommend you also choose a safeword."

"We've never had a safeword," Reolo said. "Sassafras is fine."

"That's because we don't playact." Komoko clapped Reolo on the back.

Judging from what I'd read, their activities were so dangerous that they couldn't stop in the middle.

"And please wear this at all times." I handed him a hood similar to the one that Morning wore and just as richly embroidered but made of black velvet. It seemed I'd judged the color correctly.

He put it on. "What do you think?"

"Suits you," Komoko said. "Blackhead."

"That's it! You can call me Black," Reolo said.

"Black, then."

"Killer here." Komoko tapped his broad chest.

"Lady-killer?" Daisy asked.

"Short for killer whale," Black said. "Because he's a whale."

"Better than a bird head," Killer said. "Little puffin eats too much and can't fly."

I raised my eyebrows. In making jokes, the two men had revealed their clan totems: puffin and killer whale. "Now then, Black, Morning weould like to bear a child. Daisy and I prefer to remain childless. We ask that you use barrier protection with us."

"Agreed," Black said.

"Do you have a preference for a boy or girl child?"

"Whatever she wants," Black said.

"She wants either," I said.

"Flip the coin." Black flashed a brilliant grin. "Very well. There's something you should know about me. I get an erection regularly, whenever the tide moves in the Pass, but I can't always release. It can be quite painful."

His admission confirmed our suspicions regarding his relationship to his territory. I considered assuring them of Daisy's skill, but his situation was on a larger scale than what we normally dealt with. "Gentlemen, we'll conduct you to the house, and Morning."

"I've been asked to refrain from viewing the actual act out of respect for Black and Her... and the young lady," Killer said. "We trust her completely. But I will accompany him to the door of her bower, as is traditional." He hefted a duffle bag, likely baggage belonging to Black.

"Indeed."

In a traditional wedding, the groom's witness and an honor guard of kinsmen accompanied the couple from the site of the ceremony to a secluded bower house for the honeymoon. The same custom was maintained when a man sold his services as a stud, and the transaction was euphemistically called a marriage. But the stud's witness went through the door and observed the consummation. Killer's trust shaded the relationship as a true marriage, not a business transaction or a temporary liaison.

At the door to the house, Killer bowed and said, "Tide carry you and your bride."

Black entered the sitting room and stood viewing the spiral stairway, the partly opened screen to the kitchen, and the pillow-strewn couch. "Where is she?" He twisted his bracelet, his anxiety palpable.

"Waiting for you. How do you want to meet her?" I'd been working with Morning in monthly sessions, three days at a time. Surely he deserved a similar opportunity to explore and express his preferences, but the stipulations had been clear: one day only, sunrise to sunset.

"As soon as possible," he said.

He'd misunderstood the question, so I took another tack. "She wants to give herself to you completely, so she's asked to be tied up. Is this agreeable?"

His lips parted. "Ah... sure."

"Do you need to clean up?"

By the look of him, he'd bathed recently, but I directed him to the bathroom while Daisy helped Morning. I knew what they were doing: straightening the bedspread, placing bolsters, and lighting candles.

Water gushed in the bathroom. Black returned fully dressed and wearing the hood. The black velvet covered both his braided hair and his scars but revealed his chin, lips, and dark eyes. He paced. Leaves fluttered beyond the lunette windows, sending shadows dancing on the floor.

The door opened just enough for Daisy to slip out. "She awaits within."

Black straightened his vest, touched his hood, and grasped the door lever.

# CHAPTER 11
## Offering

MORNING, MASKED IN blue velvet, lay on the bed, her skin glowing with health. Candles burned around her. Her breasts rose and fell. Black stepped inside, Seaguard from his black seaboots and life vest to the hilt of his onyx-hafted knife.

He halted and stood in awe, lips parted, gaze locked on her. "I've never seen anything so beautiful."

He knelt at the foot of the bed, bowed his velvet-covered head, and kissed her toes. She gasped. He held her leg and kissed the inside of her knee. She sighed.

On the bed, he stroked her thighs gently. "Oh my sweetness! Oh my lovely!"

She arched up against him, her soft body against his life vest and the onyx haft of his knife. He pulled off his vest and shirt then struggled with his boots. Daisy stepped forward to help pull them off, freeing his legs, and assisted in peeling off his pants.

Naked except for the hood, he lay beside Morning, stroking her belly and touching each part of her. He paused, and I knew he understood what he'd been given. He moved to get a better view. He really looked at her opening, touching each part as if memorizing it to hold it forever in his mind. He must have never experienced sex with a woman. I prayed Antares had coached him.

I gestured to Daisy, and we left the room. I was happy for Morning. Her man seemed to be what she'd wanted, what I'd wanted for her. He was tender, respectful, and appreciative. Yet I was crying. Possibly this would be only time in his life Black had sex with a woman.

There was something holy about their relationship, so Daisy and I crept out of the room and closed the door.

IN THE KITCHEN, we prepared a tray of food for our clients—strawberries, custard, oysters, rose petal jelly, salted roe on crackers.

With me peeping around her, Daisy knocked on the bedroom door. When Black gave permission, she opened it. Daisy set the tray on a side table and left. We didn't know if they fed each other or licked food off each other's bodies. They became noisy for a while. Possibly Morning was showing off her new toy. And then they were quiet. The noise began again, increasing in intensity.

"Let's go in," Daisy said.

"Wait." I held her arm. "They can hail." I pointed at my com-set.

After a time, Morning came out dressed in a robe and went to the kitchen sink to wash her phallus.

Daisy eyed the suds. "Custard pudding?"

Morning giggled. "He likes it." She returned to the

love nest, and the noise resumed.

Then Morning hailed. "We need help. Please help."

We entered. Morning was naked and standing.

Black was on the bed, his jet-tipped penis erect. He groaned, his face rigid. "Sink it! Kinkill! Poseidon take me. I can't come. I sinking can't ejaculate. Kinkill! It hurts."

"This is the problem you told me of," I asked.

"Sinking yes!"

"Daisy and I are trained professionals," I said. "May we help you?"

"For the love of Danna, yes."

"I'm going to penetrate your anus to stimulate you from behind. Is this okay?"

"Permission given. Proceed."

I stripped, strapped on my phallus, and pulled gloves and condom in place. Applying lubricant, I said, "Give me your ass."

Daisy already had a condom on his erect cock. He rolled to hands and knees. Under him, Daisy worked his penis with her mouth.

"Ready," I said.

"Aye," he answered through clenched teeth.

I pushed my phallus into his rear, taking care with the delicate tissue of his anus. I thrust at his prostate. "Come on! Come on! Give it to me. Sink you! Poseidon take you! Sink your brother! Sink your mother!" I tried for the authoritative command of Killer, but my voice came off as shrill.

With a spasm, he collapsed on Daisy. I withdrew.

"Thank you," moaned Black. "Thank you. Both of you."

Daisy emerged from under his thighs, smiling and spitting out a condom, cum on her chin. She whooped.

"Black, you are something else." She slapped his thigh.

That hadn't gone as planned. I removed my phallus and gloves. "Everybody, get dressed. Let's talk about this."

We went into the kitchen. I pulled out chairs and directed everyone to sit.

"Black, what happened in there?" I faced him across the square table, Daisy to one side and Morning to the other. Afternoon sunlight streaming through the lunette windows splashed across the surface of the table.

He scowled. "Same thing that always happens. Poseidon-damn it! Every time the tide rises in the Pass, I get a hard-on, and my damn cock gets stuck that way."

Morning slumped against the table. Beside me, Daisy fussed with the sash of her robe.

"For how long?" I asked.

"Until the bore tide passes through the Narrows—not quite four hours."

"How often does this occur?"

"Every sinking thirteen hours. I'm sorry, Morning. I lost my shot."

Good Danna! Black lived a third of his daily existence with a painful erection, and he was apologizing for not ejaculating?

"Have you spoken to a doctor about your condition?" I asked.

"Sure have. For all the good that does. They tell me if I have a patient and loving partner, I'll have no problem. They're calling it 'situational anorgasmia.' It doesn't last long enough to qualify as priapism. Frat them! It's not a medical problem."

"It's related to the Sense-net," Morning said.

"You got that right," Black said. "The Noah Code demands

that we observe the tide, and my dear addle-brained ancestors took the precept literally. They made sure I always know what the—sink it to Poseidon—tide is doing in the Narrows. Poseidon take them!"

"There must be a way to turn it off," I said.

Morning tossed her head in negation. "Once a Seaguard Lord integrates into the Sense-net, he can't be removed."

"That's not quite true," Black said with a bitter laugh. "Most clans give a failsafe to the queen, and she can remove him. Not mine. I've already contacted the queen. She was"—he shook his head—"sympathetic."

"That's horrible," Daisy said.

"Oh, it wasn't so bad at first. My 'illness' occurs during extremes of high and low tides, full and new moons, lunar conjunctions, and the summer solstice. Neap tides are okay. Killer and I are responsible for ships moving safely through the Narrows. I monitor the tide from the north and Killer from the south." He gave a pained smile. "The idea is that if I have a hard-on, ships better stay out of the area."

"How do you get anything done?" I asked. "And who is directing traffic while you're here?"

"I can delegate *some* responsibilities. We send most ships through with the moons at a quarter anyway. I've got ships moving right now." He closed his eyes. "A big hydrogen tanker just got the go-ahead."

Daisy shook her head. "So what does a baby have to do with this?"

"Uh..."

"You're here to get Morning pregnant. Yes?" she asked.

"Morning helps me out, and the payment is a child. That's the agreement. My friend Killer set it up."

"That wasn't the agreement as I understood it," Morning said. "My great-grandmother thought we'd be a good match."

I turned to the side. "Morning, do you want to have Black's child?"

"Yes, but I'd help Black regardless. I've been aware of disturbances on the Sense-net, mostly as images and feeling. My great-grandmother is trying to find a solution."

"Black," I nodded to him, "do you want Morning to bear your child?"

"Aye." He twisted the silver bracelet on his left wrist.

"Then we just need more time," I said.

"We don't have more time," Morning said. "I either conceive this full moon or never. After this, I've resolved to remain celibate."

"That's insane. No one takes vows of celibacy anymore. I've heard people did it back on Earth, but why?" Daisy shook her head.

"I've made arrangements and have obligations," Morning said. "Plenty of women have lived happily without sex."

"But not you," Daisy said. "It's not the way you are."

"Let's be strategic about this," I said. If Morning chose to become celibate, that was her choice.

Daisy paced in the kitchen. "This isn't right. It's just not right."

"But it's the way it is." Morning sat at the table facing Black. "Black and I are part of the Seaguard. Our clans singled us out as babies to receive neural implants. It's a great honor and privilege."

"A privilege? To always be alone? Never marry? Never have kids?" Daisy said.

"Not alone," Morning said. "Imagine the Sense-net as a spherical organism covering the surface of Fenria. Black and I are part of this creature. The Seaguard maintains the network, which functions as the nerves. Each cell of the organism is four-dozen to eight-dozen miles across and represents the waters monitored by a Seaguard magnate, assisted by his kinsmen. We are together in this, standing as guardians of the ocean."

"For what? Against what?" I asked.

"For the Noah Code: observe the tide, assist those in danger, be prepared. When an earthquake generates a tsunami, every Seaguardsman in the affected areas knows instantaneously. They're jolted out of sleep, even. That awareness wins us critical seconds to issue public warnings so we can move population to high ground and boats out to sea. It saves lives. So when I tell you I must remain celibate after this next new moon, believe me. It's as important as a tsunami warning. I would very much like to be pregnant with Black's child by that time."

"Black, when will you be ready to try again?" I asked.

"Not until eleven o'clock tonight," he answered.

"How important is the sunrise-to-sunset limitation?"

Morning said, "There are certain parties who don't want me to have a child. They agreed to give me a chance, provided we restrict our time together."

"But if Black stays the night, who will know?" Daisy asked.

"Initially, whomever we tell," Morning said. "But others are likely to find out tomorrow. Let's risk it."

"I'll contact the dame and let her know," I said.

Morning stiffened. "The dame?"

"Our contact," I said. "The woman who set this up."

"Please don't," Morning said. "She's one of the people who prefer I were barren. I'll talk to my... my chauffeur. Let her know."

"And I'll talk to Killer." Black put his hand to his ear. He nodded and gestured in time to his silent conversation. "Killer will meet us at the dock as if I'm leaving with him at sunset. In the twilight, the lighting will be bad for spy cameras."

"Let's make the most of our time." Black had a gleam in his eyes. "Morning, I'd love to get a good look at that cock of yours."

Morning stood, pulled her leggings to her thighs, and held up the tail of her smock. Daisy helped her pull the garment off, revealing both Morning's rounded breasts and slack penis. She wore no underwear or panties.

"Sure is a nice telechiric." He reached for it. "May I?"

Morning nodded eagerly, her eyes bright.

He grasped it with practiced confidence, lifted it to inspect the underside, then dropped it and watched it move. "Very nice. Custom-made?" He met her glance.

"Had Khyloko do the work." She stood proudly, her leggings scrunched around her knees.

"They're the best. A bit pricey though."

"I thought it might help." Morning preened. "Do you like it?"

"Very much." He licked his lips. "How long have you had it?"

"A few months."

"How are you doing with it?"

"Integration is no problem," Morning said. "I'm having trouble with differentiation."

"Differentiation is a hag. A real hag."

"What are you talking about?" Daisy asked.

He touched Morning's penis. "This is a telechiric device. Morning has taught her brain to recognize it as part of her body. That's integration. To her brain, it is her real cock. The difficult task is teaching her brain that it's different from her other part. She's got two cocks. I mean, a cock and the other part."

"Her clitoris," I offered.

"That's differentiation, and it's a hag," he said, his

hand absently stroking Morning. "The depths of it is that I've always been good at differentiation. Excuse me, ladies, I'm needed."

Morning's penis had risen in his hand.

Morning tugged at the fabric around her knees. "These. Help."

Steadying herself against Black, she lifted one leg then the other for me to remove the offending fabric. Freed of it, she straddled Black's lap. Holding her against him, he lowered his velvet-covered head to her breasts. She leaned into Black to kiss him, her lovely ass jutting toward me.

"I'll make you comfortable," he said.

He stood and, arm around her naked shoulder, propelled her into the sitting room to the couch. Daisy and I trailed behind. Among the pillows, they kissed, Morning's hand behind his fabric-covered head, gold embroidery glinting between her fingers.

I directed his hand to the base of her phallus and placed his finger over her opening. He focused on his task. His mouth descended on her erect penis. She drew her knees up, his head hidden between them.

Daisy rubbed against me. Not even bothering to remove her leggings, I reached through the split in the fabric and propelled her to a chair. Black and I pleased our women, bring them to climax at the same time. I sighed and kissed Daisy. We lay in pleasurable silence, each with our own. Beyond the walls of the cottage, birds chirped and wind sighed through distant trees.

AFTER A TIME, Daisy and I went back into the kitchen. Morning and Black joined us, his chest now bare. She wore his shirt.

I sat at the table. "About differentiation."

"Ahh. Differentiation." Black pulled out a chair and sat with Morning on his lap, his hands over hers. "Try patting your head with one hand and rubbing your belly with the other."

My right hand touching my hair, left hand on my fabric-covered belly, I patted and rubbed.

Daisy tried and declared, "Easy."

"That's because you're good at differentiation. Try this." Black divided four fingers into a V, two fingers on each side of the split. "But it wasn't always easy, no? Your brain must learn to distinguish between your fingers. Me, I've got multiple hands." He wiggled his fingers. "You don't see them because they're wireless and remotely located. Multiple feet too. No problem. I know where my hands are and which one I'm working with. But multiple wieners? That's a hag."

He squeezed Morning. "She's amazing."

Seated on his lap, Morning made a split finger V then shifted her ring finger to join with pointer and middle finger.

Daisy tried it, her fingers moving awkwardly with her pinky following her ring finger. "Oh, the time in the bathtub with the soap. Morning is good at it."

"I'm not bad," Morning said, surely an understatement. Judging from how she used a fly rod, she was phenomenal. "That's why…" She blushed. "That's why they want him, why they want us together. They predict our bab—"

Daisy planted herself in the middle of the kitchen. "I just hate that kind of genetic planning. Take two wonderful people, and all the planners care about is speed of synaptic transmission or whatever. I don't care. I don't want to care."

"I'm fucked up," Black said. "Got two wieners and can't distinguish one from the other."

Morning nudged the black velvet of his hood.

"So how are we going to solve this problem?" I looked to her.

"Tide's up tonight at quarter past ten." Black kissed her fingertips. "That's our next shot."

"What do you need?" I asked. "We got you off last time, but we... uh... missed the target, so to speak." Most of the semen had ended up on Daisy's chin.

"Usually Killer roughs me up. He comes at me from the back and—" He grimaced.

"How rough does he get?" I asked. "Bruises?"

"Sometimes." Black put his arm around Morning. "We meet on Doom Rock with the tide rising. The footing isn't very good. Last time we didn't make if back to the esskips. The bore broke over us, and we were blasted through the Narrows. Both our craft too." He lowered his head over Morning's.

"In the Narrows? At flood tide?" Morning peered up at him, her back rigid. "You could have died."

"I know. But I come when Killer roughs me up. I don't know why it works."

"I do," Morning said. "It's because we're masochists. Only a masochist would put the needs of Fenria before her own."

Daisy shook her head. "Seems unlikely. Sexual submission and political service are two different things. It could be adrenaline acting as an aphrodisiac."

"Endocrines are tricky," I said. "Particularly adrenaline. Thrill seekers often require ever greater danger to have the same effect. Such an addiction can be fatal."

"If you say so," Morning said.

"We could play it safe and repeat our earlier procedure," I said. "Daisy can use an insemination wand to deposit the fluid in Morning."

Morning grimaced.

"Or Black comes in Morning's mouth, and he makes the transfer," I said. "But we're stretching the definition of direct cover."

Black said, "My parents specified direct cover. My mother—to prevent my seed being sold on the black market. She'll not sell her grandchildren. She certainly won't let them be stolen. And according to Dad—if I can't get it up with her, I shouldn't be doing her."

"It's much simpler than all that," Morning said. "It's a differentiation problem. Black gets so much stimulation from the tide that he can't feel his own body. The signal gets swamped. Roughing someone up focuses a person on his body, not on the tide."

"We could try flogging," suggested Daisy. "Are you up for it, Black?"

# CHAPTER 13
## Flogging

I LAY OUT flogs, whips, and crops, each whip handcrafted of plaited thongs or cords, and arranged them on an occasional table. We gathered in the sitting room, all four of us topless.

"I could get used to this." Black admired the display of mammary bounty: Daisy's full breasts with wide, brown areoles, Morning's pink-tipped, and my own medium-sized. "But I've had it with these masks. Sinking things are hot." He pulled off the hood and tossed it beside the whips. "Besides, they don't fool anyone. I'd recognize Morning anywhere by the way she moves." He shook his head, and the beads braided into his hair jangled, gold against black.

Morning removed her mask as well. She smiled, and her face dimpled. "I was thinking I'd have to search for you by the color of your thingamabob. Like the prince in the fairy tale, searching for the girl with the tiny feet. Honestly, didn't he get a good look at the rest of her?"

"I'm not that difficult to find," Black said. "How many

Seaguard lords suffer erectile dysfunction caused by a tidal bore?"

"Might be one or two down in the Andean Ocean," Morning said.

I swung a whip experimentally, thongs swishing in a fall of leather. I brought the flog down on my thigh in a cascade of sound. "Done correctly, flogging is safe and effective, stinging without producing injury either physical or emotional. The most important thing—communicate with your partner. Daisy, let's show them." I gave her the flog and leaned with my hands against the wall. "Ready."

Daisy said, "I'm aiming for here, not here or here." The flog hissed as she hit her thigh, but I didn't turn to look. "This will be light, Sapph. Ready?"

The flog tickled my back.

"And medium." She struck again. "And hard."

I braced, and the whip stung. "That was a good one." I twitched my shoulders, enjoying the pleasant tingling replaced by warmth. I turned. "Flogging can produce endorphins, similar to a very hot shower. I like mine very hot. But you must be able to trust your partner. I trust Daisy, and that makes flogging fun. Ready to try?"

I handed Black the flog and had him try on his own thigh. Morning offered him her back, and he struck her, the leather falling as gently as a spring rain.

She ended up in peals of laughter. "Tickles."

"Do it like you mean it." I took the flog. "Like this. Morning, are you ready?"

She braced herself. I brought the flog down.

"Ow!" She rubbed her shoulder.

"Like that," I said handing the flog off to Black.

He shook his head, dropped the flog, and hugged her. It seemed he wouldn't strike a woman with force, even in play. And I had so feared he'd be rough with our girl.

Then he leaned against the wall and bared his back to her. She selected a whip and swung it as easily as a fly rod. She struck Black, her aim accurate and controlled. She came close, caressing him with the leather fall, tapping him, stroking him, playing him, then struck again. She was good. She could bring him to tears or make the leather into fingers of love.

WE MANACLED BLACK to the wall in the room set up as a love nest, his arms raised high, the muscles of his back and shoulders illuminated by a rosy light. Morning sat curled in a chair watching as we blocked out our activity as if it were a theatrical performance.

Black was too high, so I asked him to kneel.

"Tell me," I said, tickling his back with the flog. "Choose who will flog you."

"Morning," he said.

"And who will poke you?"

"Morning."

"And who will you fuck?"

"Morning."

"She can't do all of it." I unsnapped the cuffs and sat on the bed.

We had a problem. Ideally Morning would take three of the four roles in this play, to be both bottom and top, to both penetrate and be penetrated. But if she and Black were to conceive a child, she had to take the receptive role. I'd have to do the flogging with Daisy helping out, both of us proxies for Morning.

"Let's try another position," I said, stepping into the role of dominatrix as I blocked out our activity. "Morning, on the bed."

I positioned him over Morning then Daisy on top of him. I considered the problem. There wasn't enough room to use the flog. We'd try a different arrangement.

"Okay. Morning, turn over," I said.

Black and Daisy got out of the way, and Morning rolled over. On all fours, she peered over her shoulder as I positioned Black for rear entry. Daisy, assessing the situation and seeing her chance, slid underneath. That left me in the top position. Morning straddled Daisy. Kneeling behind Black, I rested my hand on his lower back. From this position, I could either flog him or poke him in the ass.

"Everyone okay with this?" I asked.

These were Black's methods: planning and preparation. In a strange way, we were following the Code of Noah, the ancient compact which held our civilization together. First precept: Observe the tide. Second precept: Offer hospitality to strangers in need. Third precept: Be prepared.

THE SUN SANK toward the horizon and was slipping behind the mountains when Killer hailed.

Black touched his ear. "That was Killer. He's on his way." Black went into the back and came out dressed in the clothing he'd arrived in: black pants, shirt, vest, and seaboots, the cuffs turned upward to his thighs. "I guess

I'll put this back on." He pulled the hood in place and adjusted the eyeholes and nose bridge. "Incognito."

Morning pulled her hood on as well. "We can pretend we don't know each other."

Black hefted a duffle, and the four of us walked down the path, past the boathouse, to the dock. Black indicated the boathouse with a turn of his head. "Under the eaves—a camera," he whispered.

Sure enough, the dual lenses of a binocular surveillance camera glinted in the failing light of the setting sun. We walked out on the dock, plainly in view of the camera, and waited. Black and Morning embraced as if he were truly leaving.

Killer arrived in his black-and-white esskip as the daylight faded from purple to blue dusk. "All set?" Killer stepped from wing shoulder to dock.

"Aye." Black passed the duffle to Killer and stepped aboard.

But as Killer strapped the duffle down, Black crouched and lowered himself over the gunwale on the side opposite the camera, letting himself down without a splash. Killer mounded the duffle into what could have been a person, then the canopy closed. The three of us women waved as Killer pulled away from the dock in his esskip. We walked up the path past the boathouse, knowing that Black waited under the dock.

# CHAPTER 14
## Night

WHEN THE NIGHT was full dark, before the moons had risen, Black squelched onto the veranda, dripping wet.

"Bracing," he said as he came inside.

Morning held out a towel. He rubbed his hair dry, then she nudged him onto the couch and peeled off his wet clothing and boots.

"This is more like it," he said as they settled onto the couch.

They sat together, her head on his shoulder.

MOONLIGHT SHONE THROUGH the high windows of the sitting room, illuminating Black and Morning. He set his fingers behind his ear, signaling that he was hailing. With his mouth closed and his face animate, he carried on an inaudible discussion.

He looked toward me. "Killer is back at the Pass. He's agreed to spot. I'll patch him through to the sound system if that's all right with you."

"Go ahead," I said.

"Greetings, girls," the deep voice of Antares Komoko, lord of Komoko Sound, boomed from the speakers.

Daisy laughed. "Where are you?"

"Daisy, I presume," Killer said. "On a ridge above the Narrows. It's a lovely evening. Both moons will be full. Wish I had my woman here. I tell you, Black, you have all the luck. Three beautiful women."

"Killer and I cooperate in monitoring the tide," Black said. "The bore travels south through my territory into his. He's on a ridge at the boundary with a good view looking north."

"So where do you feel it?" Killer's voice reverberated.

"Rising at Hydrogen Point."

"How long?" I asked. "Should we get undressed or have a bite to eat?" For optimal performance, we needed a break before the big event.

"I can't eat," Morning said, a hand on her stomach.

"Nervous?" I sat beside her and massaged her shoulders, sliding my hands over her bare skin, feeling for knots of tension.

She sighed and leaned into my touch.

IN THE KITCHEN, Daisy opened the cold cupboard to get cheese and salmon spread. Moonlight streamed through the window. Outside, the wind whispered through tree leaves. I stood at the window. Silver-edged clouds wafted around the moons, big round Luna Majora being chased by the nearly full little moon. Black's feet padded on the floor as he paced.

"At the Teeth." He touched his lips. "My tongue is tingling. The tide flows through me as a wave of sensation starting with my hands then my mouth."

I nodded. The tide rose to the full moons, a deep pulse that traveled unseen through the oceans. The ocean floor shaped this pulse, and in places, it rose and moved as a wave. This tidal bore drove Black's. We had to act in accordance with the tide, so we waited. Miles away, Killer waited as well, keeping his lonely watched over the Narrows.

Morning nibbled a cracker as time passed. We listened to an audio play, but none of us were interested. Daisy shut it off, and we tried charades, but that fell flat as well. So we played justice poker at the kitchen table, snapping down cards, gambling for licorice chews. Black and I played against Daisy and Morning. The goal of the game was to achieve balance with one's partner, so we'd traded partners to keep things interesting.

The cards buzzed as Daisy shuffled. Facing Black across the table, I attempted to guess at his hand and what he would play while he guessed at mine without either of us letting on to Daisy and Morning. It was a game of strategy, of bluffing, and of reading faces.

I picked up and fanned my cards. I held the grand-matriarch of wolves, the green grandmother. This card was the highest in the deck, a difficult card to balance. She'd do well with the lord of ravens. And there was always the joker. Trickster and Raven played well together. Black's dark eyes examined me over the top of his cards. With a lift of an eyebrow, I glanced toward Morning. Would he understand my signal?

His smile flashed from his eyes, too brief for the others to notice. Oh, yes, he understood. And so did I. The raven lord himself sat across from me.

We played. Black and I won a tidy pile of licorice then lost it to some brilliant plays made by Daisy. It was more licorice than any of us wanted to eat, so the loss was its own kind of balance.

Black folded his cards and touched the back of his neck. "Past the head. Killer says to get ready."

Cards put away, we returned to the love nest. Black and Morning put on their hoods. I laid out our implements on a bedside table: lubricant, cuffs, gloves, and flogs. Daisy, in a robe, sat on the bed. Morning, bolt upright on a chair, watched Black pace between the bed and the manacles on the wall. I watched all of them.

Morning stood. "Where is it?" she said, meaning the tide, I presumed.

Black stopped and pressed her hand to his heart. "Here."

Killer's deep bass reverberated from the sound system. "Not getting anything yet."

Black continued to pace, oddly like a woman in childbirth. So many times I'd kept this vigil for women giving birth—making preparations, timing contractions—caught between expectation and boredom. If all went well, we'd hold another such vigil for Morning.

"Navicular Cove." Black touched his foot. "Goes through my legs first." He stripped off his pants. "Let's get ready."

Morning and Daisy dropped their robes. I pulled off my leggings and shirt. This was the big moment.

"Fossa Shoal," Black said.

"Got it at the Cavern," Killer 's disembodied voice thundered in omnisound.

I handed gloves to Daisy, strapped on my phallus,

then pulled on a condom and my own gloves.

Killer said, "The Wrecker," which I assumed was a reef.

Black's penis rose, an arced wand, the jet tip pushing past his foreskin and nearly touching his belly. Daisy helped Morning get comfortable on the bed, placing bolsters under her shoulders to take some of the weight. I checked that a selection of whips and flogs were at hand. Daisy slid underneath, her hand coming up to caress Morning's wetness.

Black knelt on the bed behind Morning, stroking her back and rubbing his erect penis against her. He leaned forward so he was also on hands and knees, crouching over Morning, exposing his ass and balls. I moved into position and spread lubricant, and my hand touched Daisy's. The two of us worked together, helping this couple conceive. Morning moaned. Black groaned.

"This is it," Killer said.

Black slid into Morning, Daisy opening her for him. I leaned into him, my phallus against his butt, riding along his crack. I sensed their rhythm and joined it, three pelvises moving in phase, the moaning flowing together like the rush of water.

I tickled Black with a flog, playing the leather thongs over his sculpted muscles. I drew on my own jealousy. "You've been cheating on your woman." I pushed my hips into his ass. "You've been playing around with the tide." My flog struck. "You hurt Morning. I'm coming after you!" I struck again.

I took a breath. He was my tool. I'd use him to please Morning. Make love to her through him. He wasn't good enough for her. I slid my finger into his ass, easing the way, then entered with my phallus, controlling him, controlling her. Well, trying to control him, anyway

"Give it to her." I struck him with my hand. "Sink you! Give it to her. Sinking kinkiller! Down with you! Poseidon take you! Give it to her."

Black groaned through his teeth, the rasp of anguish.

In desperation, I rocked into him, but he didn't release.

"It's no good," he said. "The tide is beyond the Narrows. I'm done."

I withdrew.

He uncoupled from Morning. Daisy scooted out from underneath.

Black sat on the edge of the bed. "Once the tide passes, I go slack. Doesn't matter if I ejaculate or not."

"Maybe you could do it before the tide hits," I suggested. If he released before the rising of the tide, he'd be in a refractory state when the bore tide hit the Narrows.

Black shook his head. "We tried it. I can't get it up at all during slack tide." He gave a weak grin. "I guess that's why it's called slack tide."

"It's all right." I put my arm around him.

"Morning." He rolled away from me and reached for her.

She curled against him, comforting both of them. He stroked her head, his touch light on the embroidered fabric.

"What is Killer doing?" Daisy asked.

"Camped out," Black muttered.

I collected flogs and shut the curtain over the manacles on the wall. Daisy covered Black and Morning. We shut out the lights, closed the door softly, and went to our room.

We'd failed again.

I woke with sun streaming into our room. *Sinking overslept.* I dressed quickly and went to check on our clients. The bed was messed, Morning's robe still lay on the floor, but both our clients were gone.

# CHAPTER 15
## Ebb Tide

MY HEART HAMMERED. Had they run off?

*Calm down.* They were free to live as they wished. But what if they'd been hurt?

I went out on the veranda and onto the path. Then I saw them walking through the forest, hand in hand, light golden around them. She carried a fly rod, and he held the tackle box. She'd dressed in a smock and leggings. He wore tan pants and a hooded shirt.

"Caught breakfast," Black said, holding up a skein of trout. "She did."

"We both did," Morning said, her smile shy.

He dropped the tackle box and hugged her, fish still hanging from his hand. Happy and chattering, they came onto the veranda and into the kitchen. Black sat at the table and watched Morning prepare fish. His eyes followed her movement as if he wanted to devour her instead of the trout.

Smiling and looking at him sideways, she rolled the trout in oatmeal and placed them in the pan. When they were crisp, she brought them to him. She straddled his lap and fed him bits of the delicate flesh. His black tongue took the morsels off her fingers. Then he grasped her fingers and licked them. They kissed.

I smiled at Daisy. What a beautiful couple. If I could, I'd have saved that moment forever. Daisy and I enjoyed our share of the catch but not as much as we enjoyed watching our clients and their love for each other.

⁂

With the breakfast dishes cleared away, we sat at the table for a strategy meeting.

I leaned forward and started the discussion. "That didn't work very well."

Daisy shook her head, curls bouncing. "Too complicated."

I placed my hands on the table. "What worked? What didn't work?"

"Too much going on," Black said. "Couldn't focus."

"When is our next opportunity?" I said.

Touching his ear, Black closed his eyes. Was he tired or checking the Sense-net? "Coming up on noon."

"Let's take it easy," I said.

"All right by me," Black said. "Killer went home. Obligations."

So we went about the day as if the tide was unimportant. Daisy casually laid a throw over the daybed. We would stay away from the love nest this time.

I suggested a shave to Morning, and she accepted. Black watched with interest as she offered herself to me. I pushed her thighs open to give him a good view. With great care, I stroked the razor over her mound, between her legs to smooth her inner thighs and outer labia, then moving with care to her perineum, letting him appreciate the revelation of beauty.

I held a razor in a gloved hand. "Would you like to be next?"

He rubbed the stubble on his chin. "Maybe later."

When I had washed her with a warm cloth, he checked my work, stroking her smooth skin. She leaned into his hand. He bent and sucked, first with his whole mouth, then with just his black tongue licking the pink flesh.

When the time came, he led her to the daybed, and Daisy and I pretended not to notice. Wearing pajamas, Daisy sat curled in a chair, reading. I turned on music and attempted to crochet a doily—not that I have any use for doilies, but I had to do something. Dutifully, I counted stitches.

Black and Morning lay together on the couch, his hand moving between her legs. Then her knees were up and his head between them, surely pushing aside her telechiric penis. I imagined his black tongue exploring and touching every fold. I lost count of stitches, tangled the thread, and had to start over. Daisy dropped her screen, surely giving up her pretense of reading. Now Black was on top of Morning. She gasped—he must have penetrated.

I dropped my crocheting and stood. Daisy was standing as well. Morning held Black close as he thrust into her. Would he do it?

Daisy clenched her fist, silently cheering him on. They continued to rock.

"Come on," mouthed Daisy. "You can do it."

"Help us," Black said, his voice husky.

Daisy dropped her drawers. Underneath, she wore

a strap-on already covered with a condom. She applied lubricant then lowered herself on Black and gently pushed into him. Their hips worked in tandem, controlling double-pistons directed into Morning.

Morning arched her body, pleading for his seed, pleading to be filled. "Let me try." She pushed Black off her and moved behind him, her phallus erect.

Daisy's face lit up in understanding, and she slid under Black, reaching for his bare penis with her mouth. It wasn't a professional move, but I would have done it.

Kneeling, Morning held his hips with one hand while she pushed into him. Black came alive, twitching and moaning, serviced by two women, one with her mouth on his cock and the other massaging his anus. He spasmed and came in Daisy's mouth.

She pulled back gesturing, lips puckered, mouth full. I pulled Morning off him, and he scrambled out of the way. Morning lay among the couch cushions while Daisy delivered the semen, smearing it into Morning's delicate opening with her tongue. Good Danna, I envied Daisy.

Daisy finished. Morning sighed and brought her legs together, holding the precious and hard-won seed within her.

I pushed Daisy onto the floor, unbuckled her dildo, and set it aside. We turned head to tail, my mouth to her vagina and hers to mine. Then I realized what I was doing. I could very easily get pregnant. I turned around to kiss Daisy on her mouth. Tasting Black's seed, I probed, imagining that I was pushing it into Daisy's channel.

A light touch fingered my backside. "Sappho, may I?" Black said.

I rolled over. Daisy was now on top kissing me while

Black gently opened my legs. I gasped, his hair braids between my thighs and his soft mouth in contrast to his scratchy chin. His tongue was in me, then his finger. I arched. He rubbed faster, bringing me to climax. I gave a scream that slid into

I WENT TO take a shower and consider this turn of events. I'd never reacted to a man the way I did to Black. He was a client. He was Morning's man. And I had Daisy.

That black tongue of his was magic. But it was more than that. With his genuine smile and his tenderness, he made love like a woman.

I'd heard the tales that every girl Teakh Noahee laid fell in love with him. I'd dismissed it all as legend. Yet there I was, a confirmed Majora woman, feeling amorous toward Teakh's grandson. I was humbled.

WE WENT FOR a stroll, the four of us together. I walked between Black and Daisy, an arm around each of them and my head against Black's shoulder. To his other side walked Morning. Four of us together wasn't all that odd. Customarily, Fenrians danced as foursomes, each man with three women, and the dancers represented the forces driving the tide: earth, sun, and the two moons.

We followed the shore, walking along the shingle beach and stepping over the driftwood and seaweed cast up by the now-receding tide. Birds in the nearby spruce forest chirped. An airplane droned, not as quiet as the esskips favored by Seaguard. The sun, now in the southwest, shone on the glistening water and the snowy mountains rising from the bay.

Fenria turned about her lover, Animo, the sun. Her two lunar companions, Majora and Minora, danced attendance, the moons loving the planet and she, in turn, loving the sun. Ah yes, Majora and Minora, the lips of a woman's labia.

"You were so tempting," Black said to me with a devilish grin. "I couldn't resist."

In our foursome, I was clearly Majora, the moon of regularity. Daisy was Minora, the moon of fertility and chaos.

"Oh, look," Daisy said. She stepped over a row of flotsam to pick up a glass sphere. "An old fishing float." She held it out, the sphere still trailing the remains of hemp netting.

"By regulation," Black said, "the net rots."

The airplane cleared the ridge, a fixed-wing craft with floats below its hull.

"What the depths!" Black said.

"Kinkill!" Morning swore as the plane passed overhead.

"Come on!" Black pulled her toward the shelter of the trees.

Daisy, head thrown back and the glass sphere in her hand, looked up. "Good Danna! I believe that's the Fenrian Voyeur."

The plane turned to circle, and its tail number came into view, above it the logo of the famed scandal sheet, a spyglass superimposed over the letter Foxtrot.

"And they're landing. Let's go meet them," Daisy said.

I wasn't as enthused. "Poseidon take the scandal

sheets. What are they doing here?"

The Seaguard should have kept the media away. No craft could enter a clan's territory without clearance from the magnate. Aircraft had to file a Poseidon-damn flight plan. Failure to do so would be an inter-clan incident. Either the Fenrian Voyeur had received clearance or they'd brazenly invaded the territory of a sovereign clan.

"What fun," Daisy said. "Let's go talk to the Voyeur. We must protect the privacy of our clients."

We turned back toward the dock, and I tramped after Daisy.

When we arrived, the plane had been snubbed to the dock. Two women and a man stood beside it.

Daisy whispered, "They have hidden cameras. That's how they operate."

One of the women stepped toward us with a smile.

"Good Danna!" gushed Daisy. "I don't believe it. You must be Anisea Emmako. I'm your biggest fan. I just love your reporting. Oh, I'm sorry. Excuse my rudeness. I'm Daisy, and this is my partner Sappho. What are you about?"

"The tide," Anisea said. "We're doing a special feature on romantic hideaways."

"This is so exciting," Daisy said. "You know my partner and I have a business of arranging romantic liaisons. All for insemination purposes, of course. Would you be interested in becoming a mother? We can customize your conception experience to your unique needs."

"Fascinating," Anisea said. "So is this artificial insemination, or is a man provided? Delightful."

"However you like it," Daisy said, shamelessly flirting. "We're very good with artificial insemination."

I stepped forward. "We can assist with arrangements, but you'll have to provide the man yourself. Our business is strictly legal and ethical."

Anisea said, "So instead of going to a clinic and receiving insemination as a medical procedure, a girl can have fun getting pregnant."

"I believe treating procreation as a medical procedure disassociates sex from procreation," I said. "Sensuality, love, and childbirth are inexorably entwined and should not be divvied up between romance, marriage, and medical procedures."

"So you're saying sex is off limits unless it's to produce children."

"As long as there is love, sex is life giving. But procreation should not be without love and sensuality. A child should never be treated as an object." I felt myself shake with the passion of my belief. "At Sappho's Agency, we respect human nature and the nature of each person."

Anisea gave a little shiver. "You must work with some very interesting people. Do share with our viewers."

"No," I said. "We cannot betray the confidentiality of our clients."

"Maybe a little hint?"

I tossed my head in negation.

"We're sure you provide *excellent* service." Was she flirting with me? "Do you by chance have clients here at Cozy Cove?"

"I can't discuss that."

"That means she does," Anisea said. "We saw them as we flew in. A Seaguard man dressed in black, and with him, a woman. Clan Komoko wears black. Maybe that was a killer whale man. Could it be Antares Komoko cheating on his Fennako wife?"

Daisy said, "It's not adultery if it's within his wife's clan and with her permission."

Depths! Daisy had taken the bait and as good as admitted that Morning was Fennako. Or had Daisy played her cards well and misled Anisea?

"So a Fennako woman," exclaimed Anisea. "Who? Our viewers want to know."

# CHAPTER 17
## Bore Tide

As the Voyeur airplane flew away, Daisy and I walked up to the cottage.

"I can't believe I let that slip," Daisy said. "Founder it all. I follow her reporting. I should have seen it coming."

"It's just more rumor," I said. "You didn't say that Morning is Fennako. Anyway, Anisea is wrong about Black. She confused him with Killer."

"She'll know Black isn't Komoko when she looks at the pictures. I'm sure they took pictures when they buzzed us with the plane," Daisy said.

I touched the com-set at my shoulder and hailed Black. "They're gone. Are you okay?"

"Aye. We're having a good time."

"That was Anisea Emmako with the Fenrian Voyeur."

"I know. I planted a microphone on the dock. Seemed like a good precaution."

"I'm sorry," Daisy said.

"I'm sure Emmako already knew Morning's clan."

"How would they know?" I asked.

"The ship," Daisy said. "The scandal sheets know *Shewolf* is in the area and that the queen is aboard. They're trying to figure out what she's up to."

Black and Morning didn't arrive at the house immediately. When they did walk hand in hand onto the veranda, Morning had a birch leaf clinging to her hair. They came inside.

"You handled that very well," Black said.

"Do think they saw us?" Morning asked.

Daisy held up her handscreen. "Those pictures aren't showing up yet. Anisea is just stirring the rumors about how Antares is cheating on his wife."

"He is," Black said. "I don't like it."

"It doesn't count," Morning said. "Killer is working as Seaguard to resolve a problem on the Sense-net. It's the same as repairing a malfunctioning navigational beacon."

"So I'm a navigational beacon?" Black asked.

"My favorite beacon," Morning said.

THAT NIGHT, DAISY and I slept in our room, and Black slept with Morning. Our next opportunity: the wee hours of the night.

Black awoke me, sitting on my bed and giving me a gentle shake. "Sapph, it's time."

I yawned and rubbed my eyes. In the darkness, only a red nightlight glowed. I groped for the edge of our bed, making ready to fumble for my clothing left on a hook the night before. I felt along Black's hip, smooth and bare, and the long muscular thigh of a young man completely naked.

"Come as you are," whispered Black.

Daisy and I descended the spiral stairs in moonlight. The two moons, high and gibbous, shone through the lunette windows and cast their double shadows onto the couch in the sitting room, the cushions a mound of silver and black.

Morning was already in the love nest. She smiled at Daisy. "Wear this." She held out a harness.

"But this is yours," Daisy said. "Your little pal."

"Wear it for me." Morning buckled the harness around Daisy's waist and thighs. She rested her hand lightly on the phallus. "Black has access. We're both in here."

"You can do that?" I asked. What would it be like to share the most intimate of sensations, not just as two people touching but identical sensation? And even odder that this member could be physically separate from both of them and attached to a third person.

"Share telechirics? All the time," Morning said.

Black took command. "Daisy, you take me from behind."

"What about me?" I felt left out but silly for caring. Depths! I'd wanted one of them to become dominant. Either Black or Morning was fine.

His face flashed with a smile. "Sapph, you've got to help me. I'm juggling three wangers." He pointed to his own cock. "Get this one into Morning."

His diplomacy matched his easy command. "Just might work," I said.

"I can't handle two dicks." He laughed. "Just add one more. That'll fuck with my brain."

"It will," Morning said. "We've got to amplify sensation from Black's body. Once we get the hang of it, it should be easy to do. Black and I can make love when the tide starts to rise to release the pressure."

Black put his hand on Daisy's phallus, and I started forward. But it wasn't really hers. It belonged to Black and Morning. They both felt it.

"Getting good transmission," Black said. "Morning, how about you?" He tapped the tip.

"Distinct and clear," Morning said.

Daisy shook herself, limp penis wiggling. She cupped the member with her hand. "Such responsibility. I like it."

Morning and Black smiled, hers shy, his a flash of brilliance. They lay on each side of Daisy, both kissing her, both stroking the shared phallus. I worked my knees into the tangle of legs and reached under the prosthetic penis for Daisy's clitoris, pushing aside straps and moist skin. The three of them groaned, their sighs a chorus, Daisy soprano, Morning alto, and Black a tenor.

Black gave the word, and they changed the arrangement, Morning now on her hands and knees. I moved bolsters, assisting in positioning her. Black kneeled behind her. Daisy straddled Morning, facing backward to offer the prosthetic penis to Black. He stroked and licked, Morning groaning in time to his caresses.

Soft music issued from the speakers around the bed, activated by either Black or Morning. The beat strengthened into the complex rhythm of Fenrian surge, a dance beat.

Daisy accepted a condom and rolled it down the shaft of her strap-on, Morning's little pal. Black's own penis was erect, naked, and ready for business. Gently, I parted Morning's folds and guided Black into her. She shuddered. Blacked worked into her, hips moving in time to the music.

Daisy moved into position behind Black. I steadied him, lubed my finger, and slid it into his anus. He gasped. I held his cheeks open as Daisy pushed into him. Both Morning and Black sighed.

"Danna, that's good," Morning said.

"Oh, yes. Oh, yes." Black arched his back, pushing himself onto the robotic penis, then eased forward, pushing into Morning. "Danna, Danna. Yes."

Daisy's naked backside bumped against me. I grasped her hips, steadying her, encouraging her. As the music swelled to a crescendo, their frenzy built, Daisy riding them, driving into Black. Gasping, Morning and Black climaxed together, and the music died away.

Morning pushed the bolsters aside, and the three of them collapsed in a heap. I helped them untangle then removed the harness from Daisy and carefully set it aside on a shelf. I covered the three of them, arranged pillows, then snuggled under the covers to spoon against Morning.

"Lights out," Black said, and the room went dark.

I draped my arm over Morning, lazily rubbing her breast. She sighed, and her breath became as even as waves breaking on a sandy shore.

When I awoke, only Daisy remained beside me, her body warm and languid like a sleeping kitten's. I put my lips to her ear. "You were incredible last night."

She stretched and shrugged her shoulders. "What a thrill. We did it, didn't we?"

We climbed out of bed and pulled on robes. In the kitchen, Morning sat at the table. Behind her, the window gave view of mist not yet burned off by the rising sun. Black stood, wearing an apron and not much else, as he hulled strawberries. A teakettle steamed on the stove.

I took a cup from the drain board and spooned herbs into a strainer. I let my tea steep as I inhaled the piney scent of the herb mix.

"Do you think I'm pregnant?" Morning patted her belly.

I coughed and set my tea aside. "Implantation doesn't happen right away."

"What if I haven't ovulated?" Morning peeked at Black, her robe falling open.

"Doesn't matter," I said. "Sperm survives longer than the ovum."

"Just to be sure," Morning said with a shy smile for Black.

"Don't worry." I sipped my tea. "The day we started, you hadn't ovulated. Perfect. We planned for orgasm to cause ovulation. You were ripe for it."

Daisy said, "Sapph, you can be so dense."

I shrugged. Someone had to concern herself with the mechanics of pregnancy. Black and Morning weren't about to do it, not in their state.

"I'm game," Black said.

"Then let's do it again," Morning said.

# CHAPTER 18
## Scandal Sheets

In the afternoon, Black prepared to leave Cozy Cove dressed as an ordinary fisherman in tan pants over the tops of rubber boots. His parka was a worn but serviceable gray, and he'd covered his braided hair with a gray wool watchcap. He hefted a knapsack over his shoulder.

"Do you know where you're going?" I asked.

"I did reconnaissance on the place a few fortnights back," he said. "I'll head up the creek and over the ridge. Catch a ride from there and take the ferry home."

"You're not going without me," Morning said. "I'll hike up to the ridge with you."

When they'd left, Daisy settled in with her handscreen. I finished cleaning up after lunch.

Morning came through the door, a swing to her step. She kicked off her shoes and relaxed in an easy chair, her feet kicked up on the couch.

Daisy, seated among the cushions, held out her handscreen. "You should see the scandal sheets."

"They're such shine," Morning said.

"Who told you so?"

Morning scowled. "My mother."

"Actually, it can be fun snooping into people's lives."

"I don't like being snooped into," Morning said. "Particularly by Anisea Emmako and the Voyeur."

"It's mostly harmless." Daisy offered the screen. "Do you want to see?"

Morning flipped pages, Daisy now leaning over her shoulder.

Daisy giggled. "What a cute outfit. Sapph, what do you think? Take a look."

I chewed my lip and crossed my arms. "Okay. Let's see it."

Morning slid the screen across the table. I glanced at an image of Morning wearing a gray-green hooded tunic shot with gold, but it was nothing compared to the headline: Princess Royal to Wed. Princess Gerta Fennako and Hekho Fennako announce their engagement.

I seized the screen. Sinking god! How under Poseidon had I missed that news? What was going on?

I skimmed the article, gushing words about how the man would be the next king, about how the reclusive princess had emerged to choose a man. But the man wasn't Reolo Comryez. He wasn't her Black.

"I hate my name," Morning said, arms crossed, ignoring the obvious problem. How could Morning sit there on the couch complaining about her name after having shoved aside Black?

"You do not have to do your 'duty!' Your responsibility is to yourself," I dropped the screen. "And to the people you love."

"Calm down." Daisy seated herself in the armchair.

"I'm sure Morning has her reasons."

"What are they?" I demanded. She'd arranged to wed a man she clearly didn't love. "Are you going to wreck this man's life?" I pointed at the headline. "Are you going to wreck yours? What about your child? What about Black? Are you going to leave him in pain every day of his life?"

"Sapph, you're sounding like a radical," Daisy said.

"Well, what are you going to do about Black's problem?" I asked.

"It's not like that," Morning said. "There *is* remote sex. Both Black and I have integrated with my pal. We'll make do."

"A robotic dildo? That's a poor substitute for love."

"Do you honestly think Black would be a good king? Would he be happy?" Morning's face puckered.

"Ask him. It has to be better than what he has now. You love him. He loves you. What more do you want?"

"You're just like my great-grandmother. You think you know what I want. But you and her don't understand. What I want doesn't actually matter."

"Who is your great-grandmother?" Morning had used the word for maternal grandparent, but the mother of the previous queen was deceased. "Your father's grandmother?"

"On my mother's side," Morning said. "The queen can't keep track of everything going on—no one can—so the Sense-net has autonomous functions and emotions, intelligence. I think of this intelligence as my great-grandmother. She's very old, and she evolved in response to my ancestors, their choices and memories. She likes Black and wants us together. His problem could be her doing. I wouldn't put it past her. The Sense-net is a sly old woman. She remembers, and she plans. Right now she's planning on my marriage to Black and on our royal offspring. For a complex network, she sure can be single-minded."

"Children?" I asked.

"Survival. She was built to follow the Noah Code: observe the tide, and you will survive. She is completely dependent on the Seaguard for her survival, so she plots and plans for the type of people who will serve her well and further her aims. She fancies herself as a Poseidon-damn matchmaker, but she doesn't really care about me."

"But all living things aim to survive," I said. "This thing we call love drives us to survival. We help each other out to survive, together."

"So she set us up, sending little hints. Images, feelings, erotic dreams, even. She can jolt a man out of sleep for a tsunami. It's not any harder to increase feelings of arousal. I think that's what she did to Black. Just a nudge, a bit of amplification of sensations already there, and he's driven to fury to find release. She's not really bad. She just doesn't understand some things about people."

"So why are you marrying this prince guy?" I asked.

"My cousin Hekho," Morning said. "It's a political decision. Whomever I marry becomes king; that's the tradition. Conservatives don't like me—I'm too progressive—but they really dislike Black. He's too closely associated with both Comryez and Littlemara."

"You mean the political philosopher," I said.

"Aye. They fear that with Black as king, the real power will be either his mother, Stink Lily Comryez, or his father, Rockfish Littlemara. Hekho is much more palatable to the conservatives, and he curries favor with the Fennako City matriarchy. We reached a compromise. I have a child by Black then marry Hekho in name only. But I don't like it, and the Sense-net doesn't like it. She wants Black as king."

"Let's go into the kitchen and have some tea," I said. Serious discussion always started with mint tea, a symbol of hospitality and good will. I put a kettle on the stove, took a teapot from a shelf, and spooned dried mint into a strainer. I pulled out a chair. "Now, sit down and explain to me why Black can't be king. I think he'd make a fine leader."

Daisy joined Morning at the table, sitting beside her.

"It's horribly complicated. All these factions." Morning grimaced. "They just keep getting angrier."

I sat facing Daisy. "We just figured out how to get four people with three wieners engaged in sex—five people and four wieners if we include Killer." He'd spotted for us, but I didn't truly know how the tide affected him. "Now that was complicated. We coordinated ovulation with the tidal fluctuation in the Narrows, a tide determined by the position of two moons, the sun, and the rotation of the planet. That was complicated. Politics is simple! Some people disagree. Daisy, help us out."

At the kitchen table, the three of us prepared to discuss politics as if it were a game of justice poker or a sexual dysfunction. Maybe sexual dysfunction and politics weren't all that different. Yet the chair facing Morning remained vacant, our foursome incomplete.

I laid out the problem. "So who are these people, and what do they want?"

Daisy leaned an elbow on the table.

Morning met me with a level gaze. "There's not much you can do about it. For starters, the genetic planning committee." She flicked out her thumb for the number one. "They want a child by Black. They don't care if Black is king or not. If they had their way, everyone would be produced by artificial insemination according to their plans. All sex would be regulated or prohibited. We'd have licensed conception, and they would issue the licenses. We shall call that faction the hags. I hate them."

"Good name for them," Daisy said with a firm set of her lips.

"And then the clan matriarchs." Morning touched her forefinger to her thumb for two. "They're afraid the Seaguard will take over, that their sons and brothers won't behave themselves as loyal little lapdogs, that oh, horrors, they might fall in love, cut the apron strings, and run off with wives. Wives who have children in other clans. And the sons will fail to pay clan fees and be deadbeat uncles. Where does that leave the matriarchs? They don't want Black as king. He's too much of a radical."

"I can see why they're afraid," I said, "but not why you'd submit to them."

"The hags and matriarchs have united in their fear of Littlemara philosophy, the idea that people, particularly men, can think for themselves. That men don't need matriarchs or hags telling them what to do." Morning touched her thumb to her middle finger for three.

"About Littlemara," I said. "Have you read the philosophy?"

She nodded.

"And do you agree with it? You're going to be queen, and he called for the end of matriarchy. Are you going to abdicate?"

"I have read it," Morning said. "He calls for individual

rights. That doesn't mean ending the monarchy. My great-grandmother, not the Sense-net but my real great-grandmother, agreed with Teakh Noahee. He's always fascinated me. I wanted to be like him. It's her memory of him, which may be driving the Sense-net toward Black."

I nodded to Daisy. We'd discussed the possibility of Morning going rogue, as had Teakh Noahee. I turned to Morning. "You told me Rockfish is Reolo's father."

"He is as far as I know, but I haven't met him. I'm not sure if the philosopher actually is the same man who fathered Black."

"I've seen Black's family tree." Daisy touched her tambour screen in her pouch pocket. "His father was Sebasties Matlawko, the son of Teakh Noahee by Stellamara Matlawko, so Rockfish may very well be Sebastes Matlawko."

"Sebastes is the genus name for rockfish," Morning said, thumb still to middle finger in the sign for three. "And Maretta, or Littlemara, is a common nickname for Stellamara. It makes sense."

"I once thought that Black might be Rockfish Littlemara," I said.

"Other people think it. That's why they're afraid of him. Worst of all are the Fennako clan mothers." Morning's thumb moved to her ring finger for four. "They care only about Clan Fennako. They believe only a Fennako man is worthy of becoming king, never mind incest. To them, the other clans are provincial and insular. Never mind that they are violating the Noah Code regarding treatment of outsiders."

"I know the type," Daisy said. "The dames."

"Yes, the dames," agreed Morning. "They don't want

me to have children at all. Because if I don't, their favorite is next in line to become queen. I'm not obedient enough, not feminine enough. I'm a sinking fisheries detective. They're sure my daughter will be like me. Sometimes while I'm in Fennako City, I pack my cock just to irritate them."

Daisy laughed.

I could imagine the subtle bulge and the ensuing fuss. "But the Seaguard is behind you and Black, yes? They support the Sense-net."

"In the closet." Morning scowled. "Black really is the best. The way he works with remote devices is phenomenal, a top robotics programmer. Pretty much anyone or anything connected to the Sense-net wants Black as king. Maybe just to piss off the hags, the matriarchs, and the dames, but they want him."

"So why was this liaison supposed to be anonymous? You knew who he was, and Black isn't short on intelligence. He ran reconnaissance on this place before he arrived. Surely he knew your identity."

"The dames and the hags made that specification. They thought I could become pregnant without forming an attachment to Black." Morning snorted. "Absurd. They don't know much about the Sense-net. They pushed for artificial insemination, but Black and his family wouldn't agree. Another compromise. So what would you have me do?"

"Do what you want," I said.

"That's the problem. I don't trust my feelings. I told you about differentiation. It happens with emotions too. I can't always distinguish between my emotions and feelings from the Sense-net."

"That's a hag," I said. Danna! All this had been going on in the political world while Daisy and I had been making babies? Poor Morning had been riding this political tide. "We support whatever you choose."

AT DAWN, THE gray esskip arrived and coasted toward us. We walked with Morning to the dock. The canopy opened, revealing a male pilot. The queen hadn't come this time, probably a wise choice. The pilot stepped out and tied off then loaded Morning's gear and secured it.

"May I fly?" she asked.

"Go ahead. Your esskip."

Morning kissed and embraced Daisy. "Tide carry you."

Then she embraced me. I longed to kiss her as well, but the male pilot was watching.

"Thank you," she said to me.

"Tide carry you to good fortune."

She stepped into the esskip and buckled herself into the pilot seat. He cast off and coiled the line. The canopy closed.

"Tide carry you to love!" I shouted as Morning winged away. But where would it take her? A woman couldn't stop the rising tide, sail against the wind, or force her own heart.

# CHAPTER 19
## The Queen

DAISY AND I began the long process of breaking down equipment, packing, and lugging it all to the dock. We received a hail from Morning.

"We're having trouble with the media," she said. "Local Seaguard has a patrol guarding Cozy Cove, but when you come out, the scandalmongers will be after you. Best to move you early in the morning. We'll send esskip transport."

"What about our gear?" I asked as Daisy trundled a loaded cart onto the dock.

"How much do you have?"

Looking over the piled totes and bags, I explained.

"Won't fit in an esskip," Morning said. "We'll see what we can do."

THE NEXT HAIL came sometime between midnight and dawn.

I yawned. "Daisy, time to get up."

She murmured but remained a dark blanketed lump.

I stroked her shoulder. That got her.

She turned toward me. "But I was having such a nice dream. Six men all at once."

"And where was I in this dream?"

"Sleeping right beside me." She patted my arm, or tried to pat my arm in the darkness and got my breast instead.

I laughed. "I love you, but get up. We've got to go."

Using the dim red light, we fumbled into our clothing, left ready the evening before. We stripped the bed and stuffed sheets and blankets into a pillowcase.

The night was clear with both waning moons bright and the stars gleaming. Our baggage and gear remained on the dock.

I sat on a tote. "Sit with me, Daisy."

I put my arm around her, and she rested her head on my shoulder. Wavelets lapped the dock, and the moons kissed wave tops with their silver light. An esskip passed across the moonlit water, a shadow on the brightness—she had no running lights. The gray esskip nosed up to the dock. The canopy opened, and the pilot stood—not Morning, but the queen. She stepped onto the dock, line in hand.

"Greetings, ladies." She bowed. "Morning's mother."

"We know," Daisy said.

I elbowed her. Recognizing anyone before she identified herself was rude.

The queen said, "I suppose that makes me Night."

"Pleased to meet you." I bowed. "Sappho here. And Daisy."

"I'm sorry I don't have room for your baggage," Night said. "Local Seaguard has agreed to send it along later." She tied the line to a cleat, most likely securing the knot by feel.

"I'm concerned about the security of our baggage," I said. Someone might open a tote and see flogs and bondage cuffs, not to mention cases of condoms. I certainly didn't want to explain that to Morning's mother.

"My daughter mentioned this might be a problem. Which items are of concern?"

Night produced a red hand-light, and we found the two totes containing the flogs, cuffs, and supplies.

She snapped a lock onto each tote. "Seaguard lock. They can't be opened until you receive your baggage at your home." That meant Night knew exactly where we lived. She helped each of us into the esskip then cast off. "Seatbelts buckled?"

I fumbled for the clasp in the darkness. The canopy closed, its one-way glass nearly invisible, the stars still bright overhead.

We sped across the cove, our baggage on the moonlit dock growing smaller. I couldn't tell for sure when the esskip left the water, the flight was so smooth and silent, marred only by the nearly imperceptible pulse of the jets.

As we glided through the darkness, Night spoke. "My thanks to you ladies for all you have done. My daughter has told me about you and about Black. That's what she calls him. A fine young man. The best of the Seaguard."

"Then you'll let them be together?" Daisy said.

"If I could. As a mother, I rejoice that's she's found someone she loves, who loves her in return. But pragmatically...." she continued through the night, "I fear for them. I fear for all of us."

# CHAPTER 20
## Rockfish

Daisy and I immediately fell into bed and slept past dawn in our own house. When we woke, we ate a leisurely breakfast in the front room.

Daisy spooned cereal and yogurt into her mouth while devouring gossip news. "Listen to this." Her cheek dimpled as she glanced up from her handscreen. "'Brokered by an exclusive dating service.' That's what they're calling us. A dating service."

I licked creamy yogurt from my spoon. "Danna help us. We'll be mobbed by the lovelorn."

"They haven't got our names yet. They still think the man is Antares Komoko. Reporters have been questioning his wife and kids about adultery, but she's not talking. Oh! And this is good. Cozy Cove is a 'luxury hideaway.'" Daisy laughed. "Where are the servants? Reporters don't actually know the identity of our princess."

"What about pictures taken from the airplane?"

"You can't see much." She handed me her handscreen with a blurry image of a man dressed in black Seaguard kit. Beside him ran Morning, also a blur.

I handed the screen back to Daisy and looked up. Beyond our front window, a man stopped in the lane, his hat in his hand, his uncovered hair silver-gray. "We may have a snoop, a male snoop. Or maybe a potential client. One of the lovelorn."

Daisy glanced through the window. "He's not my type."

"Are you sure? Mature, but you know what they say about men, whiskey, and cheese."

"They get ripe." Daisy grimaced, but she had a gleam in her eye.

I stood and opened the door. "What are you about?"

He leveled his gaze at me, his eyes sultry but with crow's feet. "Are you Sappho?"

"Aye." I lifted my chin. Daisy might find him attractive, not me.

He stuffed his hat in his pocket. "They call me Rockfish Littlemara."

"That's not your real name," I said.

"Actually, it is. Close enough anyway." He smiled, an expression as genuine and fleeting as Black's bright grin. "We'll leave out my mother's clan."

"I've read your philosophy." If he truly believed what he'd written about human freedom, why had he hidden his identity?

Daisy, behind me, was all eagerness, her hands fluttering nearly as much as her eyelashes.

"That's not what I'm here about," he said. "May I come in?"

A man, or a woman for that matter, did not enter a house without stating the purpose of his visit. "What brings you here?"

"Your services." He bowed. "Let's discuss this in

private." He glanced along the street to the glass-fronted offices where several of my kinswomen were surely watching.

I sighed. Their curiosity interfered but also provided a degree of protection. I stepped back, allowing him to enter. He politely removed his shoes, and I hung his parka.

"Would you like some refreshment?" I offered.

"Please." His gaze was all over Daisy, flirting with nothing but his smoldering eyes.

She simpered then averted her glance.

"Daisy, could you bring out some of those biscuits?" I said, wishing our larder were better stocked. While he sat, I filled a cup with tea and topped it off with hot water. I held a sugar bowl and tongs. "Sweetener?"

"No, thank you."

"How can I be of assistance?" I dropped a sugar lump into my own tea and sat across from him, the table between us.

Leaving his drink untasted, he glared at me, his gaze no longer smoldering but hard. "Stay away from my son."

"Your son?" I lowered my cup. I never thought I'd be accosted by a man's father. A girl's mother, maybe.

He leaned forward. "Reolo Noahee Comryez. A client of yours."

Daisy popped back into the room. "So you're his father? For real?"

"I am unable to discuss this. Client confidentiality." I frowned at Daisy.

"Very well," Rockfish said. "Give him a call."

I'd never actually been given Black's address codes. I raised my eyebrows.

"Never mind." He tapped a com-unit. "Hailing Reolo." He leaned against the sofa back.

"Hi, Dad," Black's voice answered from the com-unit.

Rockfish lifted his teacup and raised it to me. "I'm here with a woman named Sappho. She won't talk with me. Please have a word with her."

"Put me on a com-screen," Black said.

I stood and tilted my planning screen to vertical. With a flick, I transferred the call. The pixels shifted to display Black before a wall of dark rock, seemingly inside a cavern cut into living stone. Not many places on Fenria had rock-cut architecture. He was dressed as Lord Comryez in a black-and-white life vest patterned with puffin eyes and slashes of yellow and scarlet-orange. The top of his vest revealed a gorget of plates engraved with scrimshaw drawings of puffins, the Comryez totem.

"Looks like you're home," Rockfish said.

I could see the similarity between them, the easy confidence, the assumption of command.

"What are you doing visiting Sappho?" Black asked.

Rockfish gestured with his teacup. "Finding out what you're doing as her client."

"Oh, that. Fantastic women, Sappho and Daisy. Good friends."

Rockfish stood, his teacup abandoned on my table. "Friends? Friends who have a private rendezvous during the full moon in a spawning year?"

"Dad, you're prying. I'm an adult," Black said. "And I happen to be Lord Comryez. It's my own life."

"When you father a child, it's not your life," Rockfish said, a finger punctuating his words. "It's my grandchild's life. Don't make my mistakes all over again. I sure messed up your life. Sink it all! Learn from history. I may have been a bad father. At least allow me to be an example of what not to do."

Should I have interfered in what was clearly a family dispute? Their argument must have been years in the making.

"I'm capable of messing up my own life," Black said. "Isn't that what your philosophy is about? Anyway, I have a good life."

"Do you?"

"It's the life I live. What can I say?"

"Three generations making the same fratricidal mistakes," Rockfish said, shaking a finger. "My father too—Danna guide his soul."

"You mean Teakh Noahee?" Daisy asked, barging in, all eagerness. "What did he look like?"

"About like me." Rockfish's smile flashed. "But shorter. Not as dashing as in the legends. Not dashing at all, actually. But my mother loved him. A lot of women did."

I stepped forward. "Their love wasn't a mistake." Teakh Noahee's love had produced the son in my front room and, by extension, the grandson beloved by Morning. "Love is never mistaken. Black loves Morning. It's that simple."

"Do you?" Rockfish asked of Black.

Black grinned.

"And she loves you?" Rockfish asked.

Black nodded. "That she does."

"Why can't we fall in love with the right people?" Rockfish gave Daisy a seraphic smile. "I still love his mother, Danna save me."

"Maybe we do fall in love with the right people," I said.

"That's what you wrote in your tract."

"Don't throw philosophy at me." Rockfish smiled grimly. "Not my own philosophy anyway."

Black glanced at someone off screen. "You're kidding! Really?" He flashed one of his bright smiles. "She broke it off."

Rockfish's forehead creased. "Who?"

"Morning. Uh... the princess royal. She broke off the engagement!"

Rockfish's mouth opened. Daisy whooped.

Rockfish shut his mouth. "Reolo, is that who you've fallen for?"

"She's wonderful."

Rockfish sunk into the sofa, head on his hands. "What are we going to do?"

"Offer congratulations," suggested Black.

"Princess royal of Clan Fennako?" Rockfish said. "Danna help us. Not long ago, Fennako was hunting us down."

"Morning is wonderful, and all of that is over," Black said.

Rockfish shook his head. "It won't be easy, you know."

"It never is," I said.

Rockfish straightened. "Would you let these lovely ladies know I'm not going to devour them?" His smoldering eyes included me. "Although they do look delicious. They're asking for release of confidentiality before they'll discuss the situation."

"Release given," Black said. "Signature sent. Treat my friends well."

Rockfish retrieved his tea and sat on the sofa. Black signed off, and his image faded.

Daisy bounced forward. "So you're really Rockfish Littlemara? Son of Teakh Noahee?" Eyes wide, she put her hands to her mouth.

He raised his teacup. "That's right. Sired and raised by him."

Now that was unusual. Fenrian men usually helped out with nieces and nephews and sometimes were involved with their own children, but they seldom raised children.

Daisy sat and crossed her knees, both hands set atop them, but eager for gossip all the same. "Do you know he was the most expensive stud in Fenrian history?"

I sat beside her.

"Aye," Rockfish said. "My mother paid a bundle for his services. She still claims he was worth every eulachon."

Daisy glanced at Rockfish sideways. "Have you considered working as a stud?"

Rockfish laughed. "For two such beautiful ladies, I would. But I'm married. And my wives are jealous."

"Just how many wives do you have?" Daisy said, her full attention on the man.

"Not something I talk about."

Daisy glanced at her nails. "I thought Noahee men were monogamous."

"My father monogamous?" Rockfish chuckled. "Loyal but certainly not monogamous. I was never sure how many women he actually married, but he adored every one of them."

"Oh. Ooh," Daisy said. "Then Black might…"

"Don't you be thinking that," I said. But if Morning wanted us, I'd be agreeable.

Rockfish raised an eyebrow. "Don't mess around with my son."

"You, sir"—I shook my finger—"have a huge burden of guilt. You can't unload it on Black."

"And why not? I should never have published that tract."

"Don't get your offenses confused." I put my hands on my hips. "Which do you want to feel guilty about? That as a teenager you sired a son who has matured into a fine young man? Or that you wrote the truth?"

"Neither will help him now," Rockfish said. "I gave him into servitude to Comryez. I had no choice. But now he's making the same mistake, marrying a powerful woman and giving her his child. Poseidon sink it all! I had no say in the rearing of my son."

"But he loves her," I said.

Rockfish frowned. "Because he's been primed by generations of breeding to love her. As king, he'll have even less freedom. Love and freedom? Can't have both."

"Maybe," I said. "Which do you prefer: love or freedom?"

Rockfish slumped as if deflated. "The freedom to love."

"Maybe love and freedom are the same," Daisy said, forever the optimist.

"Perhaps a person can have both." I reached for her hand. "Your son has chosen the right partner. She's tough and kind and would do anything for him. I believe in them."

"I have no illusions about Fenrian politics," Rockfish said. "They're swimming into a shark frenzy. And I— Poseidon take me—bloodied the water with my sinking tract. Sharks enraged by my philosophy."

I filled his cup with more tea. One thing for sure, Rockfish was a survivor. On a planet where most men died as adolescents or young men, he'd lived nearly long enough to become a grandfather. "Rockfish, I don't know if that's your real name or not, but you're a cagey man, alert to political tides, and smart enough to stay alive. Lashing yourself with regrets won't help

Reolo or anyone else. Think, how will you assist your son and his beloved?"

He shook his head and raised his hands, palms up. "What can I do? We are on the verge of a civil war."

"Set my net, quite a bit." I used a fishermen's idiom and narrowed my eyes. "I seem to recall your name in connection to assistance rendered to a young lady who'd lost her lover to the sea. That might have been you who helped her, or possibly she was assisted by a benefactor using your name." I tapped the edge of my cup. "I admire your courage to speak out and do what's right. Set my net, you've got many admirers. And I know for a fact that you're cagey. So you tell me."

Rockfish put his hand to his head, palm over his ear, his gesture oddly reminiscent of Black or Morning. "It's like this. The princess is an only child, no true close kin, and she has already made enemies in Fennako City. Hekho would have been the better choice for her politically, bringing two branches of the Fennako royal family together."

"The princess royal has chosen not to," I said.

"It seems she'll choose my son instead. He'll be an outsider resented by most of the royal family. I cannot help. If I'm seen around the palace, appearances will be that I'm infiltrating Fenrian politics, infecting the thinking of the royal family with my dangerous ideology."

"You have connections," I said. "Get your people in place around your son and the princess. Give them associates they can trust."

"I'm one of your admirers. You can trust us." Daisy patted Rockfish's shoulder.

"Daisy!" I said. "We must be invited."

"Would you?" Rockfish said.

"If Morning and Black wanted us with them," I said. "Good Danna! We're talking about the future king and queen, rulers of the entire planet."

"But we can always offer," Daisy said.

"Daisy!"

Rockfish bowed. "I'd be most obliged."

As ROCKFISH PASSED out of sight down the lane, Daisy rested her head on my shoulder and sighed. "So that's where Black gets his charm."

"Daisy, he's already taken, married into Comryez."

"But a girl can always enjoy the view." Daisy's eyes lit. "Come, let's see what the scandal sheets are saying." Seated, she activated her handscreen. "Oh! Oh my!" Daisy set her fingertips over her heart. "Our princess has created quite a stir."

A video clip blinked onto my planning screen. On a harbor dock, a mob of reporters shouted at a clump of royal guardsmen. The guardsmen milled, and a woman broke away from them—Morning dressed in muted Fennako green. The view zoomed in to her open collar, revealing a necklace of platinum filigree set with vibrant fire opals, the gorget of the princess royal. She flashed a brilliant smile as reporters fired questions.

"Your Highness!"

"Your Highness! What were you doing in Cozy Cove?"

"Who was there with you?"

"Does Prince Hekho know about this?"

Morning arched her eyebrows. "Why should I know or care what my cousin thinks?" She lifted her hand to push back her hair, and on her wrist, a silver bracelet flashed—Black's bracelet.

The reporters' questions became an unintelligible din, but Morning's voice rang out clearly. "Hekho Fennako is my cousin, not my fiancé." She dusted her hands. "It so happens I was trout fishing."

The din became a hubbub. Her retinue of guardsmen closed around her and hustled her through the mob. The clip ended.

Daisy sprang from her seat. "Let's pack our gear."

"Now? What for?" But I knew what she had in mind, helping Morning and Black.

"We'll go to Fennako City. We don't need permission for that." Daisy clasped her hands. "I'm sure we'll find plenty of business in the capital. You know how it is with sex and politics."

"Sex or politics? Just which do you like best?"

She lifted her shoulders. "Depends on who I'm with."

"Daisy!"

A MONTH LATER, we soaked in the bathing pool aboard the royal yacht. Morning had invited us. Black leaned against the side of the pool, a glass of fruit juice in one hand and his other arm around Morning, her head nestled against his shoulder. I relaxed beside Daisy in the warmth of the steaming water, enjoying the company.

Soft music played, quivering violins and deep cellos. Beyond broad window, sunset drenched the sea in rosy light. Daisy pushed off the bench and floated, her hair drifting like dark ribbons of kelp that swirled against my arm. Above us, a glittering tile mosaic depicted an allegory of the tides in azure and gold. The sun, a handsome man with golden hair, cavorted with three women, a perpetual dance between heavenly bodies. If Black were the sun and Morning the earth, Daisy and I were the moons that drove the tides.

Daisy dove, her buttocks rising before they sank below the surface, and she performed an underwater handstand, one foot pointing upward at the mosaic gods, her toes wiggling. Aye, Daisy was Luna Minora, the little moon of chaos and chance.

Black lifted his glass and held out his arm, welcoming me. I scooted next to him. His wet body felt good, solid and muscular.

Daisy surfaced, slicked back her hair, and pouted. "What about me?"

"Come on." Black set his drink aside.

Daisy reclined against him, her feet on my lap, her head against Morning's shoulder. Black stooped and kissed Daisy, her fingers entwined in his black hair. Morning nuzzled both of them. I massaged Daisy's toes, seeking the spot on her foot that drove her wild. Underwater, her foot twitched in my hands, and Daisy gasped.

She rotated to kiss Morning. I took a deep breath and plunged underwater. I blew bubbles, letting them rise and tickle Daisy. I surfaced to hear her laugh. The four of us floated together, caressing a thigh, a breast, a penis, the curve of a belly, enjoying whomever they belonged to and delighting in being together.

# ABOUT THE AUTHOR

**Lizzie Newell** moved to Alaska the year of the Exxon Valdez oil spill. As she traveled aboard M/V *Columbia* ferry, she fantasized that Prince William Sound was an injured boy.

The fantasy crystallized into a story when she visited Angoon, Alaska as part of an effort to install computer networks in schools. She saw the tide flowing out of Kootznahoo Inlet and knew she must write of a world where tide determines everything.

She lives in Anchorage, Alaska where she writes science fiction about the planet Fenria. She also as crafts drawings, paints, sculpture, cardmodels, costumes, and jewelry related to her fictional world.

She can be found on the web at: lizzienewell.com.

# The Fisherman
# and
# the Sperm Thief

### Prequel to Sappho's Agency

A TECHNICIAN LIFTED a vial from a rack of phlebotomy samples. The rack contained blood taken from several fishermen recuperating in the hospital.

The technician's partner leaned against a lab bench, her tawny arms crossed. "You're never going to find a good man that way."

The technician admired her Minora partner's duskiness, her skin infused with melanin as if a warm brown dye had washed through her and left behind rich deposits in her hair and eyes. They were a moon couple, Majora and Minora, two women committed to each other. To have children, a moon couple traditionally partnered with a sun couple, a man and a woman representing the sun and the earth.

"My hobby." With a pipette, the technician transferred a droplet of blood to a DNA sequencer. "The perfect father for our children." Finding such a man was nearly impossible, but the technician enjoyed the thrill of the hunt.

On a nearby wall, the five hands of a clock-calendar pointed to divisions of the hour, day, year, and periods of both moons, not yet in alignment. The Majora technician and her Minora partner still had time before the spawning tide year. Her partner snorted a laugh. "Oh, yes. Discovering an altruistic man through his genes."

"Not altruistic. Loyal!" The technician touched the screen, initiating analysis. "Noah characteristics breed true."

The partner ran her fingers through her curly black hair. "The Noah eugenics project failed."

"Maybe it didn't." The technician set aside the pipette.

"The project was disbanded. The breeding stock couldn't be controlled."

"And why couldn't Noah studs be controlled?" The technician waited as the machine ran its tests and algorithms. "I'll tell you—because they were loyal and wouldn't abandon their children. See, the characteristics breed true."

"Suppose you find such a man. What makes you think he'll cooperate when the other one wouldn't?"

The technician shrugged. "He preferred men, and that made him sinking difficult to seduce." The courtesan she'd hired to acquire the sperm had failed and returned the fee.

The partner laughed. "Searching for a four-leaf clover."

The technician kissed her Minora. "I'll find one for you, my love."

# CHAPTER 01
## The Stud

TEAKH RECLINED ON mounded pillows. A woman spooned behind him, her fingers twining in his hair and her lips on his nape, nibbling along the welts of his neuro scars. Other hands cradled his chin. The second woman kissed him, her teasing lips soft. And a third woman knelt beside his splinted ankle. Her bowed head spilled auburn hair in a cascade that tickled his thighs.

*Oh Danna! Oh Danna!* He mumbled, "I've-I've never..." How could he admit to being a virgin? A dozen-nine years old and he'd never been laid.

"That's all right. We'll take care of you."

Struggling against engulfing passion—or was it lust?—he observed details: oval nails, a hint of eye shadow, glossy hair—auburn, brown, and curly black. Courtesans maybe, but he'd never met even one courtesan, let alone been pleasured by three. These beauties were no ordinary dock prostitutes, not with every curve of pink or brown-tipped breasts and satin thighs perfect.

"I didn't get your names," he said.

"Beautiful stranger, names are unnecessary," one of them said.

The Noah Code gave highest honor to those who assisted strangers in need—anonymous charity. But other than the dull pain of his injured ankle, he wasn't in great need, and sex didn't normally constitute necessary assistance. Still, he spoke the traditional words of gratitude for charity rendered. "Honor is yours."

"We'll make you comfortable."

They settled him in the softness of the bed and resumed their ministrations. The three beauties hadn't asked permission from his clan matriarch. As for theirs, what clan held their records?

His seed was not his to share. Clan Ralko owned him. Oh, they claimed him as kin but gave him nothing. Founder them!

The auburn-haired beauty straddled him. He admired her slim waist and the flare of her hips. Her hands cupped her breasts as she arched her back and moaned, her enjoyment unmistakable.

Her skin glowed with a bright sheen as if dusted with copper. Above the rich red-brown hair of her mound, a tattoo of an angel fluttered with the undulations of the woman's midriff. Instead of legs, the angel tattoo had two fishtails curving outward like tendrils.

As if Teakh were a primitive sea sponge, he was about to scatter his sperm to the tide. He wouldn't, shouldn't, yield to animal desire, but pleasure flooded him. Impossibly, he loved all three women, loved them as Poseidon loved triune Amphitrite. To him they were sirens, irresistible.

Teakh had always hoped and expected to love one person only, as had his mother. Flouting her clan, she'd remained devoted to his father then to his father's memory. She'd often stood on a rocky headland, gazing out to sea, awaiting his return.

The sirens held Teakh in their thrall. Ah, yes. The tattoo wasn't of an angel but of a siren, one of the winged women who sang mariners to their doom.

Hands caressed between his legs—whose hands, he didn't know or care. He saw only the beauty who rode him, her glossy hair falling forward, curtaining both her face and full breasts. Then he was being kissed, intoxicated by her sensitive mouth. Heady with passion, he returned her kisses, enjoying the smoothness of her teeth, the softness of her lips. Sliding into warm wetness, he surrendered his hopes and dreams to the woman he decided to call Angel.

He and the women moaned in unison as they brought him to climax. The three were virtuosos and he was a less-than-perfect instrument, but they coaxed him to the heights of performance. He arched against Angel and, with a surge, ejaculated.

"Magnificent." She panted.

Spent, they all kissed him. He drew them close, embracing all three, nuzzling dark-ginger hair and enjoying Angel's wild, musky scent. And he wept—wept for the loss of himself as his mother had seen him and for the loss of his parents, both years dead.

Angel patted his cheek. "What's wrong?"

He had nothing to cry about. Depths! If this were the treatment for a broken ankle, he'd trip on the companionway ladder more often. Bent on extinguishing a grease fire, he'd rushed down to the galley and misjudged the last step.

"Nothing," Teakh said, but in succumbing to lust, he'd thrown away his mother's expectations. Was the taste of bliss worth it?

The woman with curly black hair spoke. "We'd best get him back to the hospital. He'll be missed."

They helped Teakh pull on his shirt, worked his trousers over his leg brace, and fastened his vest. He pulled on his one boot. They gave him his crutches and assisted him to stand.

Angel brushed her lips against his cheek. "I'll go with you."

"But you'll be seen," one of the others said, maybe the brown-haired woman. "Better he goes alone and through the back door."

Angel smiled and shrugged. "We've already been seen together."

That morning, he'd met Angel making her charitable rounds at the hospital. She'd asked about his medical evacuation. He'd claimed he wasn't a hero, and she'd laughed. They'd hit it off.

Teakh swung his crutches forward. "I'll be all right." He hoped he'd be all right. He was as new to getting around on crutches as he was to feminine favor.

A fine mist of rain spattered Teakh's face as he hobbled along the lane, passing house-front businesses. His crutches thumped the damp boardwalk. Women glanced up from planning frames placed behind the windows so they could watch the lane while working on accounting or engineering or the like.

Two pedestrians turned toward Teakh and stared. Truth be told, every head swiveled toward him, seemingly talking about him. But they couldn't have known what he'd been doing in private. There was nothing wrong with accepting the invitation of a woman during the waning moon anyway. He'd broken no laws or taboos. For all they knew, he'd only gone to get his pants repaired. Why would they care who he was? His life vest bore no indication of clan. The color, once a serviceable orange, had faded to a shade of salmon—pale dog salmon at that.

At the waterfront, men in slickers worked, cleaning decks and tinkering with propulsors. The tide had receded, and the piers now floated lower than they had in the morning. A junk scow was in, loading recyclables. A kittiwake glided, wings cupping an updraft, its mew high-pitched and plaintive. A hose gushed as a man in coveralls sprayed a boat hull. The men paid him no unusual attention, just a normal bob of the head or the greeting: "What are you about?"

Teakh gave the standard response. "Observing the tide."

That was the truth. The statement had many meanings, including engaging in recreational sex only at the proper phase of the moon. Three women dallying with one favored man at such a time was common and accepted, even expected. Dancing was traditionally done in quads, a moon couple and a sun couple. It had to be that way since women outnumbered men. Oddly though, the three beauties had avoided being seen with him.

A man pushing a wheelbarrow laughed. "Observing it nicely, I'll warrant. Or is it the girls observing you?" He winked. "I hear they're casting for you."

So strange, this sudden feminine attention. Despite the

shortage of men, women were generally picky, and Teakh was a poor relation in his clan. The name of his father's clan was unknown, and Teakh's mother had died over a dozen years ago.

At the hospital, he nodded a greeting to the nurse on duty. He entered the room he shared with Cooky, now awake and sitting up with bandages on his arm and the side of his face. The two men, injured during the same shipboard fire, had been evacuated and lodged together. The window beside Cooky's bed had been dimmed against the afternoon light, but the esskip lagoon and emergency landing could still be seen through the hazy glass.

Cooky gave Teakh a lopsided grin, half of his beard singed off. "Have a good time?"

"Aye." Teakh smiled. "Thanks."

"Thanks? What for?"

"Didn't you—" He'd assumed Cooky had arranged his encounter with the three beauties to remedy Teakh's virginity. Few on Fenria shared his mother's expectation of monogamy. No, a true mariner had a girl in every port.

"If I could get a woman like that, do you think I'd send her your way?" Cooky said.

"Three of them," Teakh said. He'd accompanied Angel from the hospital to her friend's house. The friend had a companion. The visit had stretched to include lunch then to discussion of Teakh's preferences regarding kissing. They'd ended up in the bedroom.

"I'll be sunk," Cooky said. "Some fellows have all the luck."

And that brought Teakh back to his question. Why had they gone for Teakh, an unkempt fisherman too clumsy to safely use a fire extinguisher?

He lay on his bed and activated it to elevate his foot, then he used his neuro to access the Network. He couldn't exactly search for women by hair color, and "angel tattoo" merely produced bycatch of body art and tattoo parlors.

Might as well get some other work done. Teakh hoped to establish himself as a fisheries detective, so using his neuro, he brought up video records as if to his mind's eye. Eyes closed as if he were dreaming, he viewed images of silvery pollock being pulled from the sea. Gulls screamed. He felt the boat rocking and a fresh breeze. The winch whined as it pulled the net over a squeaking block. Silver bodies spilled into the hold. Teakh focused his attention on the writhing cascade. He watched for bycatch mixed in with the target species.

A man shouted, and the camera wrenched away from the spilling fish. Two fishermen in slickers and rubber boots stood on the deck.

One lifted a finger in an obscene gesture. "Sink you, Seaguard."

This could be a prank, but more likely it was an attempt to slip illegal catch past the cameras. Teakh laughed. Fishermen were always attempting to dodge regulations, while Seaguard tried to catch them doing it. He played the game from both sides, never letting on to Cooky or their shipmates that he had a Seaguard neuro and played for the other team.

A fisherman produced a harmonica and bowed to the camera. "Here's for you."

He blew a chord, and his mate belted out a filthy ditty, the exploits of Jack Tar and his dondering dandy dickledoo. The performance ended with catcalls and hoots of laughter. The ruse was an old trick—get the enforcer focused on the bawdy antics so he'd miss what was really going on.

Teakh watched the rest of the video record in slow motion, often pausing and rewinding, searching for illegal catch that was surely there. He shifted to the other deck camera and watched again. Damn, those guys were good. Maybe their catch was entirely legal; maybe it wasn't.

He checked the records against displacement and movement of the boat, recorded at the time by underwater sensors. That seldom yielded much. He yawned. For the most part, detective work was tedious to the extreme.

"Hey! Wake up!" shouted Cooky. "Got visitors."

A nurse had entered through an open door. Two other women peered from behind her.

"Is that him? The man with the bandages?" one woman asked.

Cooky straightened up.

"No. The other one."

"He sure doesn't look like much."

Cooky grinned. "Who's the stud now?"

"You are," Teakh said. "Hey, girl. My friend here thinks you're sweeter than pie."

The women giggled, and the nurse shut the door behind her.

"We'll have none of that." The nurse advanced on Cooky and pulled the privacy curtain around his bed.

Cooky peeped out and wiggled an eyebrow. "She's changing my dressing. How good is that?"

That was Cooky, always seeing the bright side. So why were women interested in Teakh and not the more experienced Cooky? If sympathy was part of it, Cooky's injuries were worse. He had a nice full beard, or it had been full before the fire. Teakh's body was scrawny, and his sparse beard needed a trim.

Teakh went back to auditing fishing videos, attempting to find salmon hidden in cascading pollock.

The door opened. "I demand an explanation!" Aunt Dyse barged in and advanced on Teakh's hospital bed. "Oh, my dear boy, what happened to you? Are you feeling better?" She patted him, pawing at his shoulder. "What are you about?"

Aunt Dyse had never cared much for him. Her attention was the strangest of all.

"Uh, the tide," Teakh said.

"I've heard. Now tell me it's not true"—Dyse pulled up a chair—"that you were with a woman?"

"I stopped by her place," Teakh said. Aunt Dyse had no need to know what he had done in private.

"Are you sure? I won't have a bunch of hags stealing from our clan."

"She mended my pants," Teakh said. "Did a good job of it too."

"How about your seed? Where were you while she was sewing? What were you wearing? Or were you still in those pants when she did the job?"

Now that was an intriguing idea, lying in the lap of Angel as she bent over him, her needle nearly pricking his thigh. But while her companions had entertained him, she'd used a sewing machine. Then she'd used a sketch pad to draw pictures of Teakh.

"What does that matter?" he said. "The Poseidon-damn moon is waning." No child would result from his activity.

"Your seed is the most valuable thing we own." Aunt Dyse rubbed her hands. "That *you* own. We've received word that you have the Noah Code."

What was she talking about? Surely not the twelve precepts of Noah. "Auntie, I don't have a copy on me." Teakh swung his legs over the side of the bed. "But I can recite if you wish. 'Observe the tide, and you will survive. Assist those in need. Honor to those who assist strangers. Highest honor if the stranger be an enemy in need. Be prepared. Respect—'"

"The code is in your DNA."

Teakh shook his head. He supposed that if nucleic acid were treated as a four-letter alphabet, scripture could be written in a person's genes. But why? Such a text could only be read with a DNA sequencer. "The Noah Code is a lot easier to read in flagtile letters. Anyway, if it's in my DNA, I still have it. No theft occurred."

"It's not written in your DNA but programmed into you. Nephew, you've been bred, engineered even, to follow the precepts of Noah, instinctively altruistic and loyal. You are the Noah Code."

So that was the reason for women staring at him. Word had got out about his genetics, and the women thought him some sort of freak.

A guffaw issued from the other bed. "Lad, you sure have them shined."

What a sick idea, to suggest he was the result of a demented experiment. "Some joke," Teakh said. "How'd you get everyone to play along?"

"Not a joke." Dyse straightened. "For generations, scientists have sought the genetics of the perfect father, a man who puts the needs of women and children before his own. A man innately monogamous and altruistic. They tell us that's you."

Not only sick but delusional. Surely they didn't know how he earned money. "Me? I'm a fisherman when I can get the work." He passed himself off as a fisherman while investigating fisheries fraud and blackmailing poachers. For Danna's sake! He'd just had sex with three women without knowing their names. Enjoyed it too. Like depths he was monogamous.

"I don't believe it either." She shrugged. "Doesn't matter. We play this right, and we stand to pull in a good haul, make a bundle."

Sink it to Poseidon! Teakh wasn't altruistic. His investigations weren't philanthropy. Seaguard chiefs wouldn't go after the petty stuff, even after it took hours or even days to identify, so Teakh regularly went after poachers without notifying local Seaguard. He was fair, letting folks know of information in their favor, but he asked for money in exchange for withholding evidence from authorities.

"And what do I get?" he asked.

"What do you want?"

This was new. She'd never before cared about his wants and needs.

"How about my own esskip?" Teakh said. Almost every member of the Seaguard owned or had access to such a flying boat. Traditionally marine craft was purchased for a man by his mother or sister. Teakh's mother was dead, and his sister, a student less than a year his senior, couldn't afford such a gift. Without the necessary watercraft, Teakh couldn't patrol as Seaguard.

He'd made do by auditing catch records, doing

background checks, snooping around docks and processing houses, and collecting fees on his own. He'd purchased a small drone aircraft for surveillance. He'd even moved beyond his own clan's territory, working as a freelance fisheries detective. That was the title he gave himself. He hoped to develop a clientele among Seaguard enforcers in need of outside consultation. Whoever had labeled Teakh instinctively altruistic was seriously mistaken.

"You'll have your esskip," Aunt Dyse said. "But promise me"—she jabbed his chest—"never give away your seed. You talk to me before you go anywhere with a woman. We can't sell what you're giving away."

Who he had sex with was none of her damn business. Furthermore, he'd give Angel anything she wanted. If by chance she bore his child, well, that was how sex worked.

"Nothing happened," he said. Women sometimes became pregnant during a new moon in a neap tide year, but it was unlikely.

"Make sure of it." Dyse stood and stormed out of the room. Her voice came from beyond the door. "Thieves have stolen our clan property. Your protection of my nephew is completely inadequate. We demand restitution. Good Danna! He could have become ill. You call this a hospital?" She popped back into the room. "Nephew, pack your gear. I'm taking you away from all of this."

"I can't leave Cooky," Teakh said, delaying in the hopes of a chance to see Angel one last time.

"You're so sweet," Dyse said. "Always looking out for your friends. Sacrificing yourself to save another from the flames."

Anyone could use a fire extinguisher, and would most likely use it less awkwardly and more effectively than

Teakh had. Dyse flounced into the hallway.

"Sorry about my aunt," Teakh said.

"Go on," Cooky said. "Got some good nurses changing my dressing. I'll heal up. I might miss the entertainment of watching you fight off the girls, but I'll be fine."

"Well, then." Dyse glanced back into the room. "Get your gear."

"I have matters to attend to first," Teakh said.

"Do it over the Network." Dyse stood at the door.

"My comset is lousy," Teakh said for Cooky's benefit.

"I can't imagine what would require your physical presence. Actually, I can, and so we must leave."

"I'm getting a prosthetic splint," Teakh shouted. "It'll arrive in a few days." The splint would work in conjunction with his implant, speeding healing and supporting his leg while he walked normally.

Dyse waved off the issue. "Never mind that. We need to go now. You'll heal just fine without it."

"What if I refuse to go?"

"I've been appointed as your guardian. I'm only looking out for your best interest."

Sink her! If not for his sister, he'd outright refuse. The clan backed her student loan. He collected his other boot, held together with silvery repair tape. Carrying it awkwardly, he crutched into the bathroom for the toothbrush, razor, and comb provided by the hospital, the razor still unused on his growing beard. He stuffed the toiletries and extra underwear into his spare boot and was ready to go. His dummy wallet comset was in his pocket. He didn't even have a parka.

Dyse glowered and accepted the boot. Teakh couldn't carry it while on crutches.

"Hail you later," Teakh said.

"Tide carry you," Cooky said.

Teakh hobbled after Dyse, who carried his incidentals as if they were the rotting carcass of a thorny sculpin.

*The Fisherman and the Sperm Thief*

Book two in the Tales of Fenria

Now available online and in bookstores or at
**lizzienewell.com**